D0965884

Family of
Strangers

Family of Strangers

Susan Beth Pfeffer

BANTAM BOOKS

NEW YORK · TORONTO · LONDON · SYDNEY · AUCKLAND

FAMILY OF STRANGERS

A Bantam Book / April 1992

The Starfire logo is a registered trademark of Bantam Books,
a division of Bantam Doubleday Dell Publishing Group, Inc.
Registered in U.S. Patent and Trademark Office and elsewhere.

Library of Congress Cataloging-in-Publication Data

Pfeffer, Susan Beth, 1948–
    Family of strangers / Susan Beth Pfeffer.
        p.   cm.
    Summary: Through letters and essays, emotionally disturbed sixteen-
year-old Abby chronicles her growing desperation in a family
consisting of parents who seem devoid of love, one older sister bent
on self-destruction, and another older sister who has always seemed
perfect.
    ISBN 0-553-08364-3
    [1. Family problems—Fiction.   2. Emotional problems—Fiction.
3. Parent and child—Fiction.   4. Sisters—Fiction.   5. Letters—
Fiction.]   I. Title.
PZ7.P44855Fam   1992
[Fic]—dc20   91-29804
                                                                           CIP
                                                                           AC

Published simultaneously in the United States and Canada

Bantam Books are published by Bantam Books, a division of Bantam
Doubleday Dell Publishing Group, Inc. Its trademark, consisting of the
words "Bantam Books" and the portrayal of a rooster, is Registered
in U.S. Patent and Trademark Office and in other countries. Marca
Registrada. Bantam Books, 666 Fifth Avenue, New York, New York
10103.

To Mary Stolz in gratitude for her many wonderful books

Part | 1

LAST WILL AND TESTAMENT

I, Abigail Leigh Talbott, being in my right mind and all that, do hereby leave the following things to the following people.
To my oldest sister, Jocelyn, I leave my books and my CDs, and my teddy bears.
To my other sister, Jess, I leave my clothes.
Oh and I leave my jewelry to Jocelyn also.
To my mother, Ginny Talbott, I leave my furniture.
To my father, John Robert Talbott, I leave

Oct. 9
Dear Rachel,

I tried making out another will today, but I got stuck again on what to leave my father. I can never figure out what he should get. I know the will isn't legally binding anyway, nobody pays attention to the wishes of sixteen-year-olds, but I'd still like to get it all down, so people will know what I wanted them to have at least.

Of course, that's assuming I can ever figure out what I want them to have.

I left my mom my furniture this time, but that didn't feel right either. I went shopping with her for most of it, and it's more hers than mine anyway. I wanted more modern stuff. She was the one who insisted on the brass bed. She

3

told me it would last a lifetime, but who knows how long a lifetime's going to be? The way Mom made it sound, it was like my daughters' daughters would be giving birth to their daughters in that very bed, but I still would have preferred the more modern bedroom set.

You know how I am, Rachel. I never make out wills except when I'm depressed. Which I am these days. I don't know what's causing it. Fall, maybe, seeing the leaves change color and die. Jocelyn says fall is her favorite time of year, but it means school to her, and we know how well she handles that (about ten thousand times better than I ever will). I don't know what Jess's favorite season is, but I suspect it's any time after midnight.

The other thing about October is you know you're in school by then, and it feels like it's never going to end. The best you can hope for is Thanksgiving, which around here is never exactly a bundle of laughs. Dad always cries at Thanksgiving. I can't remember a single one when he didn't, even though for years I didn't know why. Sure, Jocelyn'll be back from school, and that always helps, but if Jess shows up, there'll just be fireworks, and if she doesn't show up, then Mom'll blame Dad for forbidding Jess to come home, and Jocelyn will do her peacemaking thing, and Dad'll start thinking about Johnny and start crying even sooner. That's what happened last year. Usually he holds off until halftime of the second football game, but last year, when Jess didn't come home, and Mom got so upset, he started crying before the opening kickoff.

Which has nothing to do with why I'm depressed in October, although it probably explains why November isn't my first favorite month either.

I really want this year to be better. In September I practically made a solemn vow to shape up, get my life in order, stop feeling so sad all the time. And for the first week of school, I really tried. I smiled all the time. It wasn't natural.

My jaw actually hurt after a while, and once, in the middle of the night, I woke up and I was still smiling. The smile was like carved onto my face. It was really pretty scary.

And the smiling didn't seem to make things better at school. People who had never been my friends still weren't. Nobody looked at that smile and said, "Gee, you ought to be on the cheerleading squad." They didn't even ask if my braces had just come off, and was that why I was walking around like a toothpaste commercial. They didn't notice. Nobody's ever noticed me, not at school or at home or at Girl Scout camp. I know people love me, Jocelyn does, and Mom, but even they never notice me. I bet if I called Jocelyn up right now and asked her the color of my eyes, she wouldn't know.

Hers are blue, like Mom's. Jess and I both have gray-green eyes. And Dad's eyes are sad-colored.

I wonder what color Johnny's eyes were.

Abby

October 11
Dear Abby,

Your letter came this afternoon, and I figured I'd answer it while it was still fresh in my mind. I know what Jess would say—that I'm a neurotic for being so compulsive about correspondence!—but I'm not writing to her, and I'm willing to take my chances with you. I was glad to hear school's going so well for you. You're such a bright girl, the smartest of us all, I think, although you never give yourself enough credit. I read that paper you wrote last year, and I was impressed. It was a lot better than anything I turned out my sophomore year (maybe better than anything I wrote my entire high school career). If you could just learn to relax, I'm sure your test grades would skyrocket.

5

I know—I sound like a scold. It's a bad habit of mine. It comes from years of trying to shape Jess up. I was sure a big success on that one. I know you're not Jess, and I know even if you were, you'd do whatever you want, and not pay any attention to me (after all, Jess hasn't), but bad habits are hard to break. Besides, I love you, Abby, and I want you to be happy. I know things haven't been easy for you, and sometimes when you're not looking, I catch you with the saddest expression on your face. That's when I wish I could wipe away all the pain.

You know, when you were little, you were the happiest little girl. Always smiling or laughing or singing. I know there aren't many pictures, but I have my memories, and they're of you dancing in sunbeams. Even as you got older, you still seemed the happiest of us, until Jess told you about Johnny, when you were eleven. I don't think I'll ever forgive her for doing that. She was sixteen, and old enough to know what a hurtful thing she was doing, but Jess is like that. She needs to hurt people. She hurts herself most of all, of course, but that doesn't stop her from hurting others as well.

I think what made me angriest was that Jess didn't tell you to hurt you, but to hurt Dad and Mom. You were hardly more than a bystander, as far as she was concerned, but you were the one who was devastated. I know I wasn't there, but Mom called to tell me what had happened, and I can still picture the scene. Dad angry at Jess for behaving so badly, and Jess, picking and choosing among her weapons, selects Johnny, his death, and you. She never cares who she hurts, including herself.

I'm sorry. You don't need this kind of letter from me. I don't know why I'm writing it, except I heard from Jess yesterday (don't tell Mom or Dad), and she sounded so awful, so lost and low, and there's nothing I can do for her. Part of me (a lot of me) knows that even if I could help her, she doesn't want me to. She called more to upset me than for any other reason, and she succeeded. The girl has a gift.

She asked me for money, which of course I said no to, and then she wheedled and then she begged. She was living on the streets, she claimed, no money, and none to be earned legally, and if I didn't send her some fast, she'd probably starve or end up in jail or worse (I didn't ask her what would be worse than starving or ending up in jail for fear she'd tell me). All this on a collect phone call, which I was foolish enough to accept charges for.

You know something, Abby. I am a sane and levelheaded woman, and I suspect you are too, and I look at Jess and Dad, and even at Mom sometimes, and I wonder how I could possibly share any gene code with these people.

You know something else? You are the only person I could write this letter to. My friends here think they understand when I tell them I have a crazy sister and parents that can't deal with her, but they don't know. You know. I wish for your sake you didn't, but you do, and that makes my life a lot easier.

Next letter, I promise, will be happy and cheerful and full of school news. Just like the letter you sent me.

Love,
Jocelyn

10/11
Abby—

You've got to send me some money. I'm really desperate. If I had any kind of parents, I could turn to them, but they have no hearts and neither does Jocelyn that selfish bitch. She's just like them, they don't love me and she doesn't either, but you do, you have to, because you're the

7

only person I have, and you're worth ten thousand of them, and all I need is just a little money, two hundred maybe, or more if you can spare it, and then I'll be able to straighten out my life, and get out of this dump, and start fresh somewhere, but fresh costs money, and that's why I'm writing. I know what Mom and Dad would say if I asked them, and Jocelyn has already said no in that prissy whimpering way she has, like just my asking her sullied her, but you, Abby, you know what they're like, how they can say they love you, but their eyes are dead, dead as Johnny, and I wish I was the one who'd died, and they wish it too, and you're the only one who's glad I lived and not that little brat, I'm glad he's dead, I just wish I'd died with him, I wish they all had, but they didn't and now I need money, just two hundred, or maybe more if you can spare it, and with a fresh start, I can straighten out my life, make something of myself, so they'd be proud of me, and if they were proud of me then I could spit on them for a change, and show them what they lost by not loving me.

I know what you're thinking, that that's a lot to get out of two hundred dollars, but it's a start. That's all I'm asking for Abby, is money to start, and I know you have it, I know September was your birthday, and they always give you money for your birthday, pretty bills with expensive presidents on them, and I know you never spend that money, you save it, so someday you can run away, but Abby, you should never do that, you should never run away, because the streets are hard, and you're not, you're soft, but it's a good kind of soft, gentle, like Mom used to be when she was Mommy, before Johnny died. The streets would kill you, like they're killing me, but if I only had two hundred dollars, or maybe more, I could get away from the streets, and I could live and make something of myself, and you'd be proud to call me your sister.

I have no one else I can turn to, Abby, no one else who

still loves me. Show me you love me and send me the two hundred dollars, or maybe more, and I'll show you that I really am changing, and you'll be proud of me, and we can both spit on all of them.

Jess

Oct. 13
Dear Jocelyn,

I guess you're not the only obsessive in the family, because here I am, writing back to you the very day I got your letter!

Actually, I'm writing for advice. There's a boy in school, well actually he's new, he just started in September, but he's in my history class, and his name is Tim, and that's practically the only thing I know about him, except I think he's wonderful. He's really smart, and he's cute too, but I think he's kind of shy, which is just what I need, the Outgoing Queen herself.

I want to say something to him, but I don't know where to begin or what to say, and you've always been so popular, I remember when we practically had to barricade the house, you had so many boyfriends. What should I do to get Tim to notice me, or better still to fall madly in love with me (I'm ready to skip all the preliminary stages!)?

Please be obsessive about this letter, and answer it immediately. My hormones have gone into overdrive.

Love,
Abby

9

October 15
Dear Abby,

Shyness is just nerves, and nerves come from fear of the unknown. So what you need to do is feel more in control of the situation, more like you can predict what's going to happen, and then it won't be unknown anymore, and you won't feel shy.

Write out an imaginary dialogue between you and Tim. Nothing heavy, and nothing implausible. Just you talking to him about school or where he's from, or any of the things you fantasize about talking to him about. Then once you have the dialogue written out, try it on him the next day at school. If he's shy too, he'll be relieved you started the conversation first. And if he isn't shy, he'll be flattered such a pretty girl is interested in him.

All I ask is that you name your firstborn for me!

Love,
Jocelyn

Abby: Hi Tim.
Tim: Oh, hi Abby.
Abby: I really enjoyed history class today, didn't you?
Tim: Yeah, it was great. Mr. Lopez is one of the best teachers I ever had.
Abby: Me too. I never liked history all that much before, but Mr. Lopez really makes it come alive. Sometimes I feel like I'm there, writing the Constitution with Madison and everybody else, but of course I'm not. I mean even if I was, I wouldn't be, because I'm a girl, and they were all men.

Abby: Hi Tim.
Tim: Oh, hi Abby.

10

Abby: I really enjoyed history class today, didn't you?

Tim: Yeah, it was great. Mr. Lopez is one of the best teachers I ever had.

Abby: Me too. Of course I've been in this school system forever, I mean since kindergarten, so I haven't had that much experience with other teachers. I mean, I know the kind of teachers they hire in this district, but I don't know about other districts. Other states even. Maybe all teachers are like Mr. Lopez, except I guess they aren't, since you say he's one of the best you ever had, and you just started in this district so you would know. What other teachers are like I mean in other

Abby: Hi Tim.

Tim: Abby.

Abby: I hope you don't mind my talking to you like this, just starting a conversation I mean.

Tim: Abby, I love you.

Abby: What?

Tim: I know this is sudden, and I don't expect you to love me, at least not right away, but once you get to know me, to see just how deep my love for you really is, then I hope and pray you'll give me your heart as I have given you mine. Since that very first day in Mr. Lopez's class all I've been able to think of is you. I dream of you constantly. Your face is engraved on my eyes. I yearn to touch your lips with mine, to make mad passionate love with you on the beaches of Tahiti, to write songs about you, and climb mountains with you, and when we die, we'll die together, our arms linked throughout all eternity, and other lovers will come to our graves and weep the tears that we have weeped (wept?), and share the ecstasy that the world has called ours and ours alone. Marry me, Abby.

11

Abby:

Oct. 23
Dear Rachel,

Well, what was I supposed to say? My God, I had us weeping and sharing ecstasy (which sounds kind of illegal), and I don't even know his phone number.

I guess I could have written down yes, but then I probably would have had him telling me about our kids, and the next thing you know we would have had a mortgage and two cars, and I may not be Jess, but I'm not ready to settle down quite that fast. At least not in my fantasies.

So I left his proposal unanswered.

Jocelyn (who knows me better than anybody) warned me not to do that. She specifically told me to keep the dialogue realistic, but every time I tried, I sounded as bad on paper as I do in real life. Mr. Lopez, great teacher. He isn't even that good a teacher, and for the first two weeks of class, he consistently called me Annie, which is probably what Tim thinks I'm named as a result. I should probably write out some dialogue for the two of us where I spend all my time trying to tell him I'm not named Annie after all, no matter what Mr. Lopez thinks.

You know something awful, Rachel? I had more fun writing that romantic stuff than I've had in so long I can't even remember. Even if somebody does fall in love with me someday (which I sincerely doubt), they're never going to want to make mad passionate love on the beaches of Tahiti. Get a suntan maybe, but that's it. Let alone climb mountains. Let alone me climbing a mountain. I can barely make it onto an up escalator.

I wonder if Jocelyn ever did that, wrote dialogues to give herself practice before she actually spoke to someone. I can't imagine it. Jocelyn always seems to know exactly what

12

to say to people, except me sometimes, and then only in letters. Sometimes her letters to me sound like mine to you, saying more than she should. Only it's safe when I do it, and with her it's a risk. I might turn into Jess one day, and use her letters for my own evil purposes.

Sometimes I think I'd truly be happy if I really had evil purposes.

Abby

P.S. What the hell. I'll give it one more try.

Abby: Hello Tim.
Tim: Hello Annie.
Abby: My name is Abby, Tim.
Tim: My name is Tom, Abby.
Abby: Oh.
Tim (I mean Tom): Does that disturb you, Annie?
Abby: Abby.
Tim/Tom: I mean Abby.
Abby: No. It's just when I was in kindergarten there was this really nasty boy named Tom, and I hated him.
Tim/Tom: I was that boy, Abby. I kicked you on the shin, and I pulled your hair.
Abby: And now you're back.
Tim/Tom: And I haven't changed, Annie.
Abby: You know, I should have recognized you. Tom always called me Annie.
Tim/Tom: That's because

Oct. 23
Dear Jocelyn,

Thanks for the dialogue suggestion. I've given it a couple of tries, but nothing I write comes out the way I think it's likely to (if you know what I mean).

13

Dad had a suggestion for me today, which is a real Dad idea, but I think I'm going to do it anyway. He's decided to worry that I won't get into the Ivy League school of his dreams unless I write a perfect essay for my applications. He said you had to write about the most important event in your life, so I should use the same topic, just to get a feel of it. Of course he wants to read what I write, and I don't want him to, and we would have gotten into a big fight over it, except Mom suggested that since these would be practice runs, I could do them in private, and then when I actually applied to colleges, of course Dad could read what I'd written (and make editorial suggestions).

I like the idea of practicing. I always think if I can just practice something long enough, I'll get it down perfectly, and when I actually have to do it, it won't be a disaster. That's why I liked the idea of writing possible dialogues between me and Tim, even though they turned out to be disastrous enough on their own.

Things here are fine. Mom's been unusually busy at the office lately, and Dad's had a heavy surgical schedule, so I haven't seen much of either of them lately, which is okay with me.

I'm glad you're coming home for Thanksgiving. Maybe by then I'll have actually figured out what to say to Tim.

Love,
Abby

The Most Important Event in My Life
by Abigail Talbott

The most important event in my life happened before I was born. That's the way it is sometimes,

14

the things that happen before you even exist turn out to be more important than anything that's happened since.

Here's what happened. Twenty-six months before I was born, my brother Johnny died.

I never knew him (of course). Nobody really did, since he was only two when he died of meningitis. It was one of those nobody's-fault diseases, fine one minute, dead the next, a little white coffin, funeral oration filled with angels and the love of Jesus for baby children. Innocence preserved forever. My sister Jess, who was almost four at the time, went to the funeral, and she told me all about it. She said even then she wished it was her in that little white coffin, wished she was the one Mommy and Daddy were weeping over. That's what she called them, Mommy and Daddy. I've never called them that. As long as I've known them, they've been Mom and Dad.

Jess told me once when she was about six she slipped and called Dad Daddy, and he hit her. I wouldn't believe her ordinarily, since Jess imagines a lot of hurts that never really happened, but Jocelyn, my oldest sister, said she saw it, and Dad really did hit Jess just because she called him Daddy. Johnny called him Daddy, I guess, and Mom Mommy, and they couldn't bear to hear any of their other children ever call them that again.

You may wonder why it's the most important event in my life, the death of this perfect Johnny child, Jess's maybe, but why mine, and the answer is quite simple. There wouldn't be an Abigail Leigh Talbott if John Robert Talbott Junior had lived. Why should there have been? Dad wanted a son, and he had two daughters, and finally Mom came through and Johnny was born, looking exactly like Dad, a surgeon's hands, and

15

he was precocious, oh he was precocious, which really isn't surprising, since Jocelyn is brains incarnate, and Jess is smart too, or at least she was before drugs and drink and everything else wrecked her, and I get good grades, which fools people into thinking I care about school. I don't. I don't care about anything, except maybe Jocelyn.

But Johnny would have cared. He was perfect at age two, speaking in paragraphs, running marathons, swearing to spend his life fighting poverty and disease. All this while still in diapers. He wasn't just the son Dad wanted. He was the perfect son, the perfect namesake. He would have been better at being John Robert Talbott than Dad ever was, and Dad was so in love with his creation, he wouldn't have even minded.

But Dad never had the chance. Instead Johnny packed his bags and moved in with Jesus.

Dad's no quitter. If he had one perfect son, what was to stop him from having another? Except for those nasty Xs and Ys, and the replacement child, the little replacement Johnny, was a girl instead.

A girl. Me. Whose very life exists only because Johnny's ceased. Mr. Sperm met Ms. Egg and Abigail Leigh Talbott came into being.

Sorry Dad.

Oct. 25
Dear Rachel,

Dad and Mom were both home for supper tonight, which is the first time that's happened in a while, and Dad brought up the essay I'm supposed to be practicing on. If Dad ever read the essay I wrote, I wouldn't have to worry about college applications. Ivy League schools never admit corpses.

16

I told Dad I'd tried one, but I knew I needed more practice, and then he gave me the practice practice practice lecture. You know the one: Surgeons aren't born. It takes years of studying, and even more years of practice before they can be trusted to take life into their own hands. Jess used to be able to recite the whole speech in the old days, when she was still coherent.

Mom pointed out that I still had a long time to get into shape (like a year), but Dad said my grades were "marginal" and I'd better have a great application if I wanted to get into a really fine school. I wasn't about to tell him I didn't know if I wanted to get into a really fine school, so I just nodded and said I'd try another essay real soon.

He told me to do it tonight, to write at least two essays a week until I was confident enough to show him one. I wanted to say something about homework, but of course I didn't. When Dad gets that look in his eyes, there's never anything I can say.

I decided to write to you first, and then to try another one of my Tim dialogues before I write the second essay. Compared to Jess, I'm no rebel, but I have to do something.

Abby

Abby: Hi Tim.
Tim: Oh, hi Abby.
Abby: You know, you've been going to this school for almost two months now, and I still don't know that much about you.
Tim: There's not that much to know. I have a mother and a father and an older brother and a dog. What about you?
Abby: No, we're talking about you. What do your parents do?
Tim: Dad's a justice on the United States Supreme Court, and Mom's an astronaut.

17

Abby: Gee, that's really interesting. What about your older brother?

Tim: He's in prison now, serving a life sentence for terrorist activities.

Abby: I have a sister like that. Maybe we could fix them up.

Tim: Your family sounds real interesting. Do you have any other sisters?

Abby: My oldest sister is perfect, but it doesn't run in the family.

Tim: I don't know. You seem pretty perfect to me.

Abby: My father doesn't think so.

Tim: You think you have problems? My father keeps looking at me and writing dissenting opinions.

Abby (laughing comfortably): Parents really are awful, aren't they?

Tim: My mother the astronaut is pretty nice. Of course she's in deep space a lot of the time.

Abby: So's my mother, and she never leaves earth.

Tim: So it's you and your parents and your two sisters?

Abby: I had a brother once, but he died before I was born.

Tim: What was he like?

Abby: He was the most perfect one of all.

Tim: He sounds great. I'm sorry I'll never have a chance to meet him.

Abby: No sorrier than I.

Tim: Maybe we could go to his grave site someday, lay flowers there, talk about who he would have been if he'd only managed to survive.

Abby: It's a date.

Tim: I'll give you a call next week, and we can find out what hours the cemetery is open.

Abby: Oh Tim, you're so romantic.

Tim: I can't help it. Just looking at you makes me think of dead babies.

The Most Important Event in My Life
by Abigail Talbott

I am the youngest of three sisters. My oldest sister, Jocelyn, is seven years older than me, and my next oldest sister, Jess, is five years older than me. There used to be a little boy, Johnny, but he died, and this isn't about him.

When I was seven, my father got very angry at my sister Jess. It seemed like he was always angry at her about something or another. Jocelyn says Jess likes to have Dad angry at her, but I don't see why she would, since Dad's really scary when he's angry.

This time, when Dad got angry, I was there. The fight started over what we were going to watch on TV. This was a completely unnecessary fight, since Jess had a TV set in her room, and so, for that matter, did Dad. But Jess was on the couch in the family room, and Dad came in and changed the channel. I was watching TV with Jess at the time, but this fight wasn't about what I wanted to watch. I don't think they even knew I was there after a while.

It was a Saturday afternoon, and Jess was watching some stupid comedy on cable, and Dad walked in and changed the channel to a basketball game. Jess (not unreasonably) got angry at Dad for doing that, only she made the mistake of telling him so, rather than just leaving the room, going to hers, and watching her show there. Once Jess told Dad she was mad, he got even madder, and soon they were screaming at each other, shouting all kinds of names, and you couldn't really tell that one of them was a grown-up. At first I thought it was kind of funny. I was used to seeing Dad mad at Jess, but this time he seemed like such a baby. I remember thinking the kids at school shouted a lot like Dad when they called each other crybaby and dummy.

Dad told Jess to leave the room (I don't think he cared whether I stayed or went), and Jess refused to get up, so Dad walked over to the couch and lifted her off of it. Then Jess kicked Dad in the leg as she walked away, and that really got Dad going. He walloped Jess, hit her so hard she fell halfway across the room, and then he started shaking his hand (he's a surgeon) and screaming she could have cost him his career, and Jess got up and just lunged at him, and I thought they were going to kill each other, so I started screaming, and Jocelyn came in. I don't know where Mom was.

Jocelyn pulled Jess off of Dad and shoved her out of the room. Dad kept screaming, shouting all kinds of bad names at Jess, who was screaming back and crying and striking out at Jocelyn. But Jocelyn never lost her calm, just pushed Jess into her bedroom and slammed the door on her. Of course, most of that I couldn't see from where I was, cowering on the couch, terrified Dad would notice me and think somehow all this was my fault.

But he never did. He never once seemed to see me. I was seven years old, I wasn't tiny or invisible, but Dad was so angry at Jess, I might as well not have been there. He was shaking his hand, and then he walked over to the TV set, lifted it up and threw it onto the floor. It kind of exploded when it landed, the picture tube shattered, and one of the pieces of broken glass flew toward me and cut my arm.

But I was too terrified to move, or even cry out. I thought if I did, Dad would kill me. So I stood absolutely still, and watched the blood start dripping on my shirt.

20

Dad left the room, went to the garage, got in his car, and drove away. When we all knew he was gone, Jocelyn went back to the family room and got me out of there. She got Mom, and they put a Band-Aid on my cut. It really wasn't a bad cut, more scary than painful.

Mom and Jocelyn threw the TV set out together, and Mom went out and bought a new set, so when Dad came home, there was one waiting for him. She took Jess with her, and when she came back without Jess, I thought she'd dumped her someplace, the same place she'd left the TV, but she'd taken Jess to her sister's instead, and Jess spent the rest of the weekend there. She came home after school on Monday, but Dad stayed at the hospital really late that night, and by Tuesday, they weren't fighting anymore.

I learned a lot that day. I learned just how angry Dad could get, and that you couldn't count on Mom to step in and stop things. But mostly I learned I might as well not exist. Not even Jocelyn saw me when she pulled Jess out.

I also learned it wasn't necessarily bad not to exist. At least Dad never got mad at me the way he did at Jess, and I wasn't expected to face him and save the day, the way Jocelyn was.

So from that day until today, I've hardly said a word. Oh sure, I talk when I'm supposed to. But Dad isn't home that much, and lately neither is Mom, and when they are, they seem to find my silence appropriate. I try very hard not to be a bother. I get the grades Dad wants me to, and I make as little fuss as possible at home, and I behave myself all the time. I'll never be Jocelyn, and I'll certainly never be Johnny, but at least I'll never be Jess, and if Dad doesn't love me, the way he does Jocelyn and Johnny, at least he doesn't hate me, the way he hates Jess.

21

When I grow up, I'd like to be a scribe. I'd like to work in a well-lit room, sunshine pouring in, the walls white and unadorned, and I'll sit all alone, crouched over an oak plank table, copying in a beautiful hand words of ancient wisdom.

10/29
Abby,

I could really use a hundred dollars. Just a hundred and I can get into a detox center, they won't take you if you don't have a hundred. That's the entrance fee. With a hundred dollars, they promise they'll get all the poisons out of your system, and once they're gone, then everything will be all right.

I know it's asking a lot of you to send me a hundred dollars, but I don't have anybody else to ask. Aunt Martha and Uncle Mike are no longer speaking to me, and Jocelyn just sends me sermons when I ask her.

It occurred to me that you might not want to send a hundred of your own dollars to me, and I can't say I blame you, as I'm not exactly a great credit risk these days, but I had an idea. Mom and Dad always leave money lying around the house. Dad keeps five one-hundred-dollar bills in the toe of his left hiking boot, and he never checks to see if they're still there. I know because I used to take the money out and put it back just to see. If I'd only had a little more time when I left for good I would have taken the five hundred with me, but nobody gave me two weeks' notice.

Even if you don't want to risk taking one of the hundred-dollar bills from there, there's still other money lying around. Mom keeps some in the freezer, and she keeps at least a hundred in her black sequin evening bag, and Dad usually has a twenty in his razor kit. So there are a lot of

22

places you could take the money from and they'd never notice, or you could wake up early and take some money from their wallets, not so much that they'd notice, but twenty from one, thirty from the other, and then you can supplement from the evening bag and the razor kit, and before you know it I'd have my hundred.

I bet you're asking now why you should take the risk, but they'll never suspect you. They'll think I slipped in one night and stole the money, and in a way they'll be right. You can even say you saw me, that I threatened to hurt you if you told them I broke in. It won't matter. Even if they want to press charges, they won't be able to find me. Besides, once I finish at the detox center, I'll be clean and I'll tell them that's why I needed the money, and they'll be so happy, they won't care that I broke in and stole it.

You know, since you're taking all that money anyway, and blaming me, you might as well throw in a couple of hundreds from Dad's boot. The detox center only costs a hundred, but I'm sure I'll have expenses once I get out, new clothes to go on job interviews in, and a decent room to stay in. Take as much as you can, and send it to me, and I promise you I'll take the blame and turn my life around and make you proud of me.

Jess

October 30
Dear Abby,

Remember how Dad used to say he never worked as hard as he did in medical school? He was right. I feel like all I ever do is work, which of course can't possibly be true.

Still, I love the challenge, and the idea of being a doctor excites me so much. I'm afraid I'm going to disappoint Dad by not going into surgery, but I want a specialization that

23

allows me more involvement with the lives of my patients. Right now I'm favoring oncology, but of course I still have time to change my mind a few dozen times!

It was funny reading how Dad's making you write sample essays. He made me do the same thing. It didn't matter that I was class valedictorian, etc. He wanted me to have the perfect essay. He wrote me one, as a sample for me to practice with. His topic was the most significant person in his life, and he wrote about Granddad, so I obviously was supposed to write about Dad, which I did. Dad's the most important person in my life anyway, so it wasn't like I needed the hint.

Sometimes I think about how I'll be the fourth generation of doctors in the Talbott family, and I picture Granddad writing an essay about the most important person in his life, and writing about his father. I wish I could remember Granddad better. Dad idolized him so. Dad told me once the proudest moment of his life was the day he got his medical degree and his father attended graduation to see it. According to Dad, that was the only time Granddad went to any of his graduations. Doctors' schedules and all that.

I wrote all those wonderful practice essays about Dad, and then it turned out Yale wanted an essay on the most important event in my life, for which I was completely unprepared. Dad and I racked our brains trying to think of just what that event could have been. To be perfectly honest, I wanted to write about Johnny's funeral, since it was there I decided to be a doctor, so I could cure little children and make Dad miss Johnny just a little bit less, but I didn't have the courage to tell Dad that. Besides, he wanted me to write about some accomplishment of mine. My tenth-grade science project, or the summer I spent as an exchange student, something like that.

It was Mom who finally came up with my topic. She said I should write about my work at the senior citizens home,

24

and the time Mrs. Cook gave me her Bible the day before she died. Dad thought it was "too soft" but Mom convinced him it would show Yale what a well-rounded person I was, doing volunteer work and all that. I got into Yale, so I guess Mom was right.

It's a good thing Jess never got around to applying to colleges. I shudder to think what she would have picked as her most important event. I wonder what yours will be.

Have I ever told you how much I love writing these letters to you? I don't even know if you read them all the way through. But when I write to you, I don't have to think about skeletal systems and digestive tracts and endless enzymes. I know Jess would never believe it, but some of my happiest memories are of home and my family, and our letters back and forth let me know that those connections remain strong and unwavering.

Love,
Jocelyn

The Most Important Event in My Life
by Abigail Talbott

When I was eleven years old, I got drunk. It was on a Friday evening, and my parents were out. I thought they were together, at a party or something, but it turned out my father had had to stay at the hospital because of an emergency, and my mother had gone out for dinner with friends of hers.

I was alone that evening. My sister Jocelyn was at Yale, and my other sister Jess had run away from home for the first time a couple of weeks before. I guess she'd already called home once or

25

twice, since I don't remember anybody really worrying about her.

I would tell you about why Jess ran away, but that wasn't the most important event in my life. It might have been in hers, but she isn't writing this essay.

There's a wet bar in the family room, and I walked over to it and poured myself a quarter glass of gin. I filled the rest of the glass with Coke. It tasted awful, but I kept sipping at it until I'd finally finished it, and then I poured myself some vodka and Coke and drank that all the way down. My parents drink, and Jess certainly does, and even Jocelyn has a glass of wine with dinner, so I figured there had to be something to this liquor business.

After the vodka, I poured myself some rum (and Coke), but I couldn't get that all the way down. First I threw up, and then I passed out, and when I came to, Mom was cradling me, rubbing my face with a cold washcloth, and begging me to get up, so she could clean the room before Dad got home and saw me.

I was groggy at first, but then I knew exactly what she meant, and I sobered right up. I even helped her clean up my vomit. By the time Dad got home, I was asleep in my room and the family room had been so thoroughly Lysoled and aired out, he never knew what I had done.

That was the most important moment in my life because Mom protected me and showed me what would happen if I continued to behave that way. I can't say I never drank again, but I never got drunk, and I don't think I ever will. I'm not Jess. I couldn't survive the way she has.

I could never succeed at success the way Jocelyn has. But I could never succeed at failure as well as Jess either.

I'm glad I learned that when I was eleven. It saved me a lot of heartbreak.

Nov. 2
Dear Jocelyn,

Of course I read your letters all the way through. I practically memorize them, I read them so often. I love reading about what you went through when you were my age. As a matter of fact, I just wrote another one of those practice essays on the most important event in my life (I wrote about something you probably never knew I did—how I got drunk when I was eleven). I thought about changing my topic to the most important person in my life (I would have picked you), but since Dad hasn't told me to change topics, I figured I'd better stick to the one he wants.

Don't worry. I know I can't send Yale (or any other good school) an essay about getting drunk when I was eleven. It probably wasn't even the most important event in my life. I just like writing the kinds of essays Dad wouldn't approve of. When it comes time for me to write the real one, I'll pick something good I did, and write about that instead.

School's fine. Dad wants me to get my grades up this year, so I'm working extra hard, and it's paying off. My last history grade was a 97 (my average last year was 93), and that in spite of being distracted all the time by

LAST WILL AND TESTAMENT

I, Abigail Leigh Talbott, aged sixteen and two months, do leave the following things to the following people.

To my sister Jocelyn, I leave my books and CDs.

To my mother, Ginny Talbott, I leave my clothes and my shoes.

To my sister Jessica I leave everything else, all my jewelry, and my money, my stocks and bonds and whatever is in my trust fund, and the twelve dollars and thirty-two cents in my pocketbook, and the three hundred and fourteen dollars and nine cents in my savings account, plus whatever interest is in there that they haven't marked down.

To my father, John R. Talbott, I leave

Nov. 2
Dear Rachel,

I was in my room, writing to Jocelyn, when Dad came in to see what I was doing. He didn't even knock. He never used to knock when he went into Jess's room either, and that was the first thing I thought of, that he never knocked when he went into Jess's room.

He demanded to know what I was doing, so I told him the truth, that I was writing a letter to Jocelyn, and he insisted on seeing it, only I couldn't show it to him, and he said that I was supposed to be writing one of my practice essays, and I told him I already had, and he said in that case why wasn't I doing some homework, and I told him I'd already finished my homework (which was true), and he made me show him my homework, so I did. He said I should show him my essay next, but I couldn't. It was about something I did he never knew about, and he was in a bad enough mood already. So I stood there and told him it hadn't turned out the way I'd wanted, and I'd thrown it out.

He got mad then, and said if I didn't concentrate I'd never get anywhere in life, that I wasn't naturally gifted the way Jocelyn was, that I'd have to work for everything I ever got, and the only chance I had to get into a good college and make something of myself was if I worked and worked and worked and never wasted a single minute on essays I knew I couldn't submit.

I must have blushed really hard then, because he pressed his advantage. I was goofing off, wasn't I, writing things just for my own amusement, wasting my time, wasting everybody else's time, and now I was wasting Jocelyn's time too. Didn't I know what hard work medical school was, even for a girl as brilliant as Jocelyn? Why was I bothering her with my stupid letters? Was I trying to drag her down to my level? If mediocrity was all I could hope for, would I only be happy if she was mediocre too?

When Dad gets into one of those moods, there's nothing I can say, so I just sat there, trying to hide my essay and my letter, because I was still scared he'd demand to read them, and then he'd move from Jocelyn to Jess and I'd be lost.

But Dad lost interest in me almost as fast as he'd gotten it, and he stormed out of the room, after telling me a couple of times I'd be lucky to get into a community college with my aptitude and attitude.

I shook for a while after he left, because it always scares me so when Dad notices me. At first he shouted at Mom about what a disappointment his children were to him, even Jocelyn was wasting her time, but then he went into the family room and turned on the TV.

29

Mom kind of tiptoed in here then, which was nice of her, and she told me not to pay any attention to Dad. He'd lost a patient today, someone who never had much of a chance anyway, but Dad hates it when they die on him (all good doctors do), and November is a hard time for him anyway. Of course Dad knows how hard I work, and he's really very proud of me, and so was she, and everything was going to be all right.

I can't remember the last time Mom talked that long to me.

I told her I knew all that, and it was okay, and I really did understand Dad, and how much he wanted me to do all right with life, and not be like Jess, and Mom got that hurt look she always gets when someone mentions Jess. She said Jess had willfully chosen to destroy her life, and of course I would never do anything like that, I wasn't even remotely like Jess, which I know I'm not, but I was a little surprised to find out Mom knew too.

I asked Mom then if it was okay for me to keep writing to Jocelyn, and she thought about it and said I should probably cut down on my letters, because Dad was right, medical school was a lot of work, and the fewer distractions Jocelyn had the better. She said no matter what, I should never complain to Jocelyn, or even suggest that I was unhappy, because Jocelyn had been through enough worrying about Jess, and she shouldn't have to worry about me too. It wouldn't be fair to her. So I promised her I'd stop writing Jocelyn so much.

I wish I had a friend, a real friend, someone I could call right now, someone who would know who is sane and who is crazy, and would tell me, and I would know to believe her. I'd give them all up, even Jocelyn, for one real friend.

Abby

30

Abby: Hi Tim.

Tim: Oh, hi Abby.

Abby: Are you ever lonely, Tim? Do you ever wish there was someone you could reach out to, someone who knows the whole story, someone who likes you for who you are, cares about you, maybe even loves you?

Tim: Abby, I don't know you very well.

Abby: But do you want to know me? Do you want to care?

Tim: I'm the oldest of thirteen children, Abby. I go to school all day, and then I go to work at the foundry. Every spare minute I have is spent earning just another penny to keep my family from starving. As well as football practice, violin lessons, volunteer work at the hospital, and being an Eagle Scout.

Abby: I guess you are kind of busy.

Tim: Too busy for you.

Abby: Hi Tim.

Tim: Oh, hi Abby.

Abby: I'd like to be your friend, Tim.

Tim: Get lost.

Nov. 4
Dear Jocelyn,

You may wonder why you haven't heard from me in a while. That's because I've been forbidden to write to you. Well, that isn't exactly true. I'm not supposed to write to you so much. I'm a distraction to you. The important thing is for you to do well in med school.

I'm not surprised they think of me as a distraction. That's actually the most they've thought of me ever, I think.

Anyway, I don't think they'd mind if I write you letters, just as long as I don't mail them. They don't care if I'm distracted, just as long as my grades go up and I keep on writing those practice essays.

31

The thing is, when I write to you Jocelyn, half my letters are lies. Nice lies, happy ones, about how well I'm doing, and how great things are at home, and it just seems like a waste of time to write those lies if you're never going to get to read them. It isn't like I'm fooling myself.

So what's the point? I've never confided in you the way you think I have. I've never told you everything. You don't know that Jess writes to me regularly begging me for money. You don't know that my life consists of nothing—studying, hiding, writing letters and essays and practice dialogues for conversations I'll never have. Wills. I write my will out too, Jocelyn, a new one every couple of weeks. You don't know any of that, because I never wanted you to, because I never wanted it to be true. I wanted what I wrote you to be the truth, those things-here-are-fine letters, those thanks-for-the-helpful-hints notes.

I wish Johnny had lived. I wish I'd been born anyway, some accident of contraception, or even another shot at a baby boy (insurance for the loss of the precious son), but I wish Johnny had never moved up to heaven, that he was here for Dad to love and Mom to acknowledge.

I wish I had red hair and blazing green eyes, and a poodle.

Love,
Abby

LAST WILL AND TESTAMENT

I, Abigail Leigh Talbott, leave everything, my books and CDs and furniture and teddy bears and notes and letters and practice essays and dialogues, and whatever money I may have to Tim Flannery, so he might notice me after death as he never has in life.

Abby—

I'm going to be staying late at work tonight. Take something from the freezer for your supper. Dad'll be eating at the hospital.

Mom

Mom—

Some man called and when I answered he asked if you were in. When I said you weren't he hung up without giving me his name.

Abby

The Most Important Event in My Life
by Abigail Talbott

The most important event in my life might not seem all that important to anybody else. I guess that's how it is with the really important things. It's the lesser stuff, assassinations and wars, that everybody believes count for something.

When I was ten years old, my family went on a picnic. All of us. It was a Sunday afternoon, and Dad took his beeper with him, just in case he was needed at the hospital, but it never beeped once that whole afternoon. We got in the station wagon (Mom's car), which Dad hated driving in, and Mom packed us a picnic lunch of sandwiches and salads, and we drove for about an hour to park grounds somewhere in the country, and found a picnic table, and spread our meal out and ate it.

There was a stream nearby, and Dad and Jess and I walked over there. Jocelyn stayed back with Mom. Dad held Jess's hand and mine, she got his left,

I got his right, and he told us about how he went fishing once with his father, who was also a doctor, someone even busier than Dad. They'd gone fishing that one time, and Granddad had told Dad all about being a doctor, and how much he looked forward to seeing Dad become one. I said I'd like to be a doctor too, and Dad laughed, and said there could never be too many Talbotts in medicine. He even asked Jess what she wanted to do. She looked so pleased to be asked. Jess flunked everything, she'd practically made a life's work of failure, but when she said she wasn't sure, but maybe she'd like to be a reporter, Dad didn't laugh or tell her she could never get into a decent college with her grades or say her brain was already so addled she couldn't report on anything. He just said that sounded really interesting, and maybe she should work on her school paper. I remember Jess asked him if he'd ever thought about being a reporter, and he laughed, but nicely, and he said he'd always known he was going to be a doctor, but Mom liked to write, and Jess must have gotten it from her. And Jess looked back, and she could see Mom sitting and talking with Jocelyn, and she smiled. I could feel that smile like a charge of electricity, the current running from Jess, through Dad, to me. My arm tingled, and I smiled too.

We must have looked so normal, the three of us walking together, talking and smiling, and holding hands. I wanted other people to see us, to admire the perfect family scene. I wanted pictures, videos, an oil painting of me and my family, having a picnic, talking and smiling. I wanted that moment to last forever, its sweetness like candy, like honey, like wine.

On the drive home Jocelyn started singing Row

34

Row Row Your Boat, and we all joined in, harmonizing as best we could. I can still hear the echoes of our voices, and I know that day is a part of me, a part that no matter what, I'll never lose.

November 6
Dear Abby,

What's up? It feels like an awfully long time since I heard from you last. Is school keeping you that busy or have you started dating Tim, and that's all you're thinking about?

I have to admit I wish I was involved with someone right now. I know things would never have worked out between Roger and me, but I miss him sometimes, just the way he held me on nights when I felt so alone. I think about him, wondering what he's up to. I never should have broken it off so completely. I do that too often, just cut things (I mean people) off. I guess I look at Mom and Dad, see what happens when you hold on, and panic.

I need to get letters from you, Abby. I need to know things are good with you. Your letters remind me there's a real world out there, that I have connections. I can't lose that.

Write soon.

Love,
Jocelyn

Nov. 9
Dear Rachel,

Jocelyn knows something's the matter. I got a letter from her today, and it was filled with what's-going-on questions, demands that I write to her, admissions of vulnerability and longing.

I don't know why she does that to me. The only way I can manage is if I think of Jocelyn as steely perfection. Let's face it. The rest of my family is a mess. Dad and Mom both manage their jobs successfully, but that's about all, and Jess is best left undiscussed, and Johnny is I'm sure great as an angel, but not much good on earth, and as for me, I can't even manage to make up a conversation with a boy, let alone actually conduct one.

I'm waiting for Mom to tell me Dad no longer minds if I write to Jocelyn. I'm scared to write to her before then, scared Dad'll find out and take it out on me. My best chance at survival is to keep him from noticing me. I have Jess's eyes.

Abby

Nov. 11
Dear Jocelyn,

I don't know what you've heard from Mom and Dad, or even if they've told you anything, but I figured you'd like to hear what actually happened, so when you come home for Thanksgiving you'll have a better idea of what's going on.

I went to bed last night early, and neither Dad nor Mom was back by then. Mom's been working almost as much as Dad lately; I guess I've told you I haven't seen much of either of them. Anyway, I was alone in the house when I heard a noise. At first I thought it was Mom (Dad's sound I can recognize), but there was something not quite right. Rubber-soled shoes, a kind of sneaky silence.

For a moment I panicked, and thought it was robbers, and nearly called the police. But then I heard a voice whispering my name, and I realized it was Jess, so I went out to the living room.

She looked awful. I've never seen her that thin, and she looked like she hadn't bathed in days. Her hair was long and stringy, and her eyes dominated her face. She was just eyes and sunken cheeks, and her breath was foul.

She said she needed money, she was desperate for money, and she had nowhere else to turn. I asked her how she'd gotten here, and she said she'd hitched, but I don't think anyone would have picked her up, the way she looked and smelled. I told her we were alone and she said she knew some places where Dad hid money, and she'd just take some and leave.

I followed her into Dad and Mom's bedroom, and she went right to the closet, found one of Dad's hiding places, and took two hundred dollars. I didn't know whether I should stop her. I was pretty sure I could, if I just pushed her or something, she seemed so fragile, but I was afraid she'd break if I did, and it seemed more important to me that she get out of there before Mom and Dad got back.

But when I told her she should go, she just laughed, and she walked with me to my room, sat down on my bed, asked me how things were going. I figured if she was there already, I could at least feed her, but she said no, she wasn't hungry. Jocelyn, she looked like she was starving, but I couldn't force-feed her. Besides, the longer she stayed, the more nervous I got.

Mom showed up first, which I think was a disappointment for Jess. She went out into the living room, and as soon as Mom saw her, she began to cry. Then she took a deep

37

breath and told Jess she had to get out of there before Dad came home.

Jess said why, it was her home too, wasn't it, and Mom said Jess knew she wasn't welcome in it until she straightened herself out and proved to all of us that she was worthy of our trust. Jess started laughing then, and she showed Mom the two hundred dollars and said if she couldn't have their trust, at least she could have their money. Mom got really hysterical then, begged Jess to leave, but it was too late. We could hear Dad's car pull into the driveway.

Mom practically pushed Jess to the front door, figuring Dad would come in through the kitchen, but for some reason he came in through the front, so of course he saw Jess. It was awful. He grabbed Jess and shoved her outside. He said he'd call the police if she wasn't off his property in thirty seconds.

Jess just stood there laughing, and Dad slammed the door in her face, but you could tell she hadn't left, she was just on the front steps laughing at him. Dad picked up the phone and dialed 911 and asked for the police, but before he had a chance to give the address, Mom hung the phone up. She shouted at Dad, begging him not to make a scandal. I really couldn't tell whether she was protecting Jess or her own reputation, but I guess it doesn't matter. Dad left the room, went to the family room, and slammed the door. He spent the rest of the night there.

Mom wouldn't open the door for Jess, even though she rang the bell for an hour, and knocked on the door, and begged us to let her in. Eventually she gave up and left. Mom wouldn't leave the living room until she did. I think she was afraid I'd open the door for Jess if I were left alone.

The next morning Mom got up and acted as though nothing had happened. Dad slept late (in the family room), and when he got up he asked if Jess was still there. When we told him she wasn't, he said good, and took a shower. I pretended to go to school, but once I was sure they were both gone, I went back into the house (feeling like Jess, feeling like I was sneaking in) and tried to get some sleep. After a while, I gave up, and began this letter to you.

I wish Jess had taken more money. It doesn't seem right somehow that she was on the front steps all that time and only ended up with two hundred dollars.

Can't wait to see you at Thanksgiving. We all need you so much right now.

Love,
Abby

Nov. 11
Dear Rachel,

I just sent Jocelyn a letter about what happened last night, but of course I didn't tell her everything, and I really feel like I have to write it down somewhere.

Sure, I got most of the details down straight, but not everything. I couldn't tell her everything, it just wouldn't be fair.

I guess what upset me the most (except for seeing Dad's absolutely unwavering rejection of Jess, and how Mom backed him up, no matter what she wanted) was what Jess said to me when we were alone in my room.

I know this is crazy. I mean, Jess looked awful, like walking death, and I had the strongest sensation I might never see her again, she might actually die before she ever gets her life straightened out, and that wasn't even what upset me so much.

It was Jess saying one of those casually cruel things she used to say all the time. I can't remember a time

39

when Jess wasn't saying something hideous about some-one, but she never lied. I never wanted to hear what she was going to say because I always knew it would be the truth, and the truth is something I'm not always comfort-able with.

We were sitting on my bed, two sisters sharing midnight confidences, and Jess was asking me how everybody was, almost as though she cared. I know she doesn't. Jess was always mean to me. I can think of maybe a half a dozen times when she was nice. My earliest memory of Jess is her twisting my arm and laughing at me. Jess really is as awful as Dad says she is. The problem is he's just as awful as she is.

So there we are on the bed, and Jess is asking how we all are, like she cares, and I say Dad and Mom are both real busy, as always, and Jess just laughs. "I wonder who it is now," she says, so I ask her what she means, and she laughs even harder, and says don't I know, half the time when Mom claims to be working late, she's with a man?

I told her she was crazy, and she grinned and said I was right, it wasn't half the time, it was at least three-quarters, and she couldn't blame Mom, if she were married to Dad she'd cheat every chance she could get, and she couldn't believe I hadn't figured that out yet. Sure, Jocelyn might not know, but I was a lot smarter than Jocelyn ever was, and I must have realized a long time ago that nobody worked as hard as Mom claimed to.

I felt as though she had punched me. It's funny, isn't it. I'm not exactly a hotbed of illusions where this family is concerned. I figured out a long time ago we were all crazy, except maybe Jocelyn, and sometimes I think anybody as sane as she is must be crazy too. Mom has hardly been home in weeks. And this isn't the first time she's hardly been home.

40

Everything collapsed when Jocelyn went to college. Up until then, no matter how bad things were, we pretty much stuck together. But Jocelyn was hardly gone for a month before Jess ran away, and even though she came back that time, she ran away twice more before Dad finally told her never to come back. And Mom started spending more and more time at work, and of course Dad's never been home, not really. I don't think I can remember having supper three nights in a row with him, unless he's been on vacation.

It just never occurred to me Jess wasn't the only one running away. Of course it would be Jess who'd tell me. Jess just loves being the bearer of bad tidings.

I wonder if it's true. Jess made it sound so plausible that I have to think it's a lie. Her brain is warped from drugs and liquor and hate (hate first, then liquor and drugs). Can walking death even know the truth?

I wonder if I'll ever have the nerve to ask Mom. No, that's silly. I can barely make myself ask her to pick up some milk. I'm not about to start confronting her on questions of marriage and morality.

Abby

Abby: Hi Tim.

Tim: Oh, hi Abby.

Abby: What do you think about fidelity?

Tim: A great virtue. One of the all-time best. Without fidelity, there can be no trust, and without trust, no love.

Abby: Means that much to you, huh?

Tim: Are you suggesting it shouldn't?

Abby: No. I don't know what I'm suggesting.

Tim: What can be more sacred than the marriage vows? Do you mean to suggest forsaking all others only covers occasions when you're not really interested anyway?

Abby: But lots of people commit adultery.

Tim: And that justifies it?

Abby: But what about forgiveness?

Tim: That's between the husband and the wife. It's not the daughter's place to forgive.

Abby: Can the daughter understand?

Tim: By understand you mean forgive.

Abby: So what if I do?

Tim: Do you understand Jess?

Abby: What do you mean?

Tim: Do you look at Jess and see what happens to a child who's met with nothing but callous rejection, or do you see a mess, a half-dead creature always cruel, never loving, wanting only to hurt and demanding only to be hurt in return?

Abby: I see my sister.

Tim: You see your worst fears.

Abby: And when I look at Mom, what should I see?

Tim: A woman who lives fully only when she's away from those she's supposed to be loving. A woman who's happiest when she's in the act of betrayal.

Abby: And when I look at you, what do I see?

Tim: You see yourself. I am nothing but a mirror.

November 14
Dear Abby,

I just got your letter. It was the first I'd heard of it. Naturally Dad wouldn't want me to know—you know how he is about distractions.

I'd come home right away if you thought it would do any good, but I have a feeling we'd all be better off if I came home on schedule and pretended not to know anything. Dad or Mom might confide in me in person, but as long as

42

they're not telling me, I can only assume they don't want me to know.

Which is not the same as saying I don't want to know. I'm grateful to you for giving me the report. Jess is my sister, no matter how crazy she may be, and sometimes I think she's going to die and I'll never know. She'll just vanish one night on the streets, drugs killing her, directly or through disease, or maybe she'll provoke one fight too many and somebody will kill her. I'd love to say I can predict a happy future for her, but I can't. For you I can, and for me, but never for Jess.

I wish you were in college already. I wish you were away from home, making a life of your own. I know you think high school was a breeze for me, but I'm no fool, I knew things were horrible, and all I wanted was to do what I should and leave.

I'm sorry. My mood is dark these days, and your letter, which I really was glad to get, has only made me feel worse.

Sometimes I envy Jess. It's hard always doing right, being scared sometimes to face the consequences of coming up short, not being perfect. Of course Jess has perfected failure. God forbid she should ever come up short on that, get a job, cleanse her body and her soul.

I know you'll find this hard to believe, but in many ways you've been sheltered, Abby. I only wish you could have been protected just a little better, just a little longer.

Call me if you need me.

Love,
Jocelyn

11/14
Abby—

Having a wonderful time. Wish more of Dad's money were here.

Jess

The Most Important Event in My Life
by Abigail Talbott

When I was six years old, I met my older brother Johnny for the first and last time.

Under any circumstances, that would have been unusual, but since Johnny had been dead for eight years, it was really unexpected.

I was homesick. It was the only time in my life I've ever been seriously sick, and at that, it was only a virus, but a mean one, and I was running a fever of 103. My mother actually stayed home from work to be with me, which I really liked. She'd started working after Johnny died, and she loved her job, so she always spent a lot of time there. Or at least that's what I'd been led to believe.

But I was sick, burning with fever and all that, so Mom stayed home to nurse me. My father, the doctor, was at the hospital, busy saving other people's lives. Not that mine was in jeopardy. I guess he peeked in on me, but I don't remember that. What I remember is Mom, sitting on my bed, wiping my brow, reading out loud to me.

My older sisters, Jocelyn and Jess, were nice to me too. Jocelyn sat with me, telling me stories, and Jess bought me a doll and told me we'd play with it together when I got better. We didn't, but it was still nice of her to say we would.

So mostly I liked being sick, although not enough to get sick again. It was more attention than I was used to, and attention turned out to be nice, which was something of a surprise.

But at first, when the virus hit, I didn't feel well enough to enjoy any of the perks. I remember thinking that I wanted to die. I was half asleep one day, or maybe it was night, feeling awful beyond description, when I saw a little burst of light come through my bedroom window. It took all my energy, but I forced myself to concentrate on it, until I could see it was a little baby.

I wasn't immediately worried about why a baby had materialized through my closed window. I remember being more concerned that I didn't know if it was a boy baby or a girl. The baby was dressed all in white. Now that I have a little more experience with babies, I'd say it was about a year old.

When the baby spoke, it said, "Hello Abby," and it spoke in a deep, man's voice, so I knew it was a boy. I said hi back, and asked if it was the baby Jesus. I couldn't figure out who else might be visiting.

45

The baby laughed. "No, I'm your brother Johnny," he said. "But I know Jesus, and He loves you with all His heart."

I was glad to hear that. "Will he bring me presents?" I asked.

Johnny laughed. "That's Santa Claus," he said. "He loves you too."

I remembered then the difference between Jesus and Santa Claus and felt embarrassed. But it didn't matter. I really liked this talking baby floating in the room. He finally settled down about a foot above my chest of drawers, so I had to look up to see him. I sensed he liked having that advantage over me.

"How do you know Jesus?" I asked, although I was a good deal more interested in Santa.

"I live with Him in the kingdom of heaven," Johnny replied. "I live there with millions of other little babies that He saw fit to summon to Him."

I nodded, although I had no idea what summon meant. I thought it might have something to do with summer, and I pictured all the millions of babies swimming at the ocean with Jesus and Santa.

"Do little girls live there too?" I asked. It was the end of November, and winter had set in early that year. I missed the ocean and the shore.

"Not with the babies," Johnny said. "Heaven's very big. Little children, children your age, live someplace else, but Jesus visits them every day too."

I remember resenting the fact that this baby thought of me as a little child. You don't expect to be condescended to by someone in diapers.

"Am I going to go to heaven?" I asked.

Johnny nodded. He looked funny, floating over the chest of drawers, his head bobbing as he nodded.

46

"Now?" I asked. I didn't want to, since my class had a trip planned to the firehouse the following week, and Mom had sworn to me if I was well enough, I'd get to go.

"Do you want to go now?" Johnny asked.

"No," I said. I started crying then, thinking he would take me even if I didn't want to go.

"Do you love Mommy and Daddy?" he asked.

"Sure," I said. I did, too.

"And Jocelyn?" he asked.

"I love Jocelyn," I said.

"Do you love even Jess?" he asked.

That was when I knew he wasn't lying about who he was. Only my brother would know how hard it was to love Jess.

"Most of the time," I said. I didn't think even Jesus could love Jess all the time.

"And do you love your teachers and your classmates and the birds in the trees and the flowers of the field?" Johnny asked.

Johnny certainly asked a lot of questions for a little baby. I began worrying he was a front man for Santa, and this had nothing to do with heaven and everything to do with presents.

"I've been a good girl," I said.

"I know you have," Johnny said. "I watch over you from heaven. I'm very proud of you, Abby."

"I want to go swimming," I said.

Johnny flew over to me, swooped down, and kissed me on my forehead. "When you're well, you'll go swimming," he said. "Someday, when you're old enough, you'll go swimming forever."

I liked the way his kiss felt, cool against my fevered brow. "Tell Santa I've been good," I said, hardly able to keep my eyes open.

47

"Do you send Jesus your love?" Johnny asked.

"I love Jesus," I replied. I was afraid sending love meant getting an envelope and putting a stamp on it, and I hadn't done that much in my life, and was nervous I wouldn't know how.

"Jesus and all the babies in heaven love you too," Johnny said. I had a strong sensation of his looking down on me, committing me to memory, but then he floated away from the bed, back toward the window, and was gone.

I have never told anybody about this visit from Johnny. For starters, I didn't know there had been a Johnny until I was eleven, and my sister Jess told me. I'd always known something was wrong in my family, some secret kept, but I was being protected from the truth, as though keeping me from knowing would keep me alive.

And then, when Jess told me, and the little floating visitor made sense, I didn't think I should tell anyone. If Johnny had wanted to get in touch with anyone else, he knew where to materialize. His visit had been something between him and me, and I chose to keep it that way.

But what the hell. If writing about it will get me into Yale, why keep it secret?

Nov. 17
Dear Jocelyn,

Just a note to let you know things are a lot calmer around here, and I can't wait to see you at Thanksgiving.

I got an A plus on a paper I wrote for English. Even Dad was impressed.

48

And in history class, Tim asked if he could look at my notes from the day before (when he'd been absent). Be still my heart!

See you in a week.

Love,
Abby

Tim: Hi Abby.

Abby: Oh, hi Tim.

Tim: Those were great notes you took in history class.

Abby: Thanks. I work very hard at writing good notes. My academic standing is quite important to me.

Tim: I know. That's what excites me most about you.

Abby: Excites?

Tim: Whenever I see you in class, scribbling notes, occasionally glancing at the blackboard, I am consumed with a raging passion. It's all I can do to keep from grabbing you, carrying you out of the classroom, out of the school building, and ravishing your exquisite body in the parking lot.

Abby: I don't know much about these things, but do we have to do it in the parking lot?

Tim: Where would you rather be ravished?

Abby: Paris.

Tim: Paris it is then. Any place you want, my studious beauty.

Abby: You know, I like it when you go first in these practice dialogues.

Tim: I wish you had told me. I would have been happy to go first from the beginning.

Abby: That's the story of my life. I'm just a natural leader, fighting to get into the spotlight.

Tim: You occupy the spotlight of my heart already.

Nov. 19
Dear Rachel,

Give me a break. The spotlight of my heart? I have to admit though, I liked the part about ravishing my exquisite body.

All things considered, I'm feeling quite cheerful these days. I love the idea of seeing Jocelyn, even if it's just for a long weekend. I'm sure Jess will stay away and I don't think Mom's going to be distraught over her absence. And maybe this year, Dad'll forget to get weepy over Johnny, and we might even make it through Thanksgiving dinner like ordinary people.

Or, barring that, at least make it to halftime of the second game.

Besides, things are going well at school. There's something about getting an A plus on a paper that really boosts your confidence. And Tim did ask to see my notes. It's true, I sit next to him, and he probably picked me just because I was convenient, but there might have been more to it than that. Mike Schultz sits on Tim's right, and he didn't ask him for his notes.

Rachel, there are moments when I can actually picture being happy, not necessarily now, but in some perfect future. Somebody loves me in that future, a man who kisses me whenever he sees me, someone who holds me when I cry. Sometimes I even think I'll have children. I'd like a son, a real baby Johnny to nurse and nurture. And a house, an old one with gingerbread and a big front porch, and two dogs, and a cat that sleeps in the sunlight.

You want to know the truth? This image comes complete with aprons and the smell of baking bread. I wouldn't recognize the smell of baking bread if it hit me, but I bet it smells like love.

50

However, even in this most perfect of worlds, nobody says I'm the spotlight of their heart!

Abby

11/20
Abby—

Two hundred dollars just doesn't last as long as I thought it would. I was an idiot not to take more when I could, but I guess I was hoping when Mom and Dad saw me, they'd offer me more, more than money, a home, love, apple pie, a car, redemption.

Anyway, here's the deal. Take a quick trip to Dad's boot, see if he's replaced his hundreds, and if he hasn't, send me what's left. If he has, then he's keeping an eye on it, and you'd do better to check out Mom's bag and the razor kit.

Wherever you get the money, send it to me immediately. Otherwise, I might feel the need to pay another visit home, this time in time for the turkey and stuffing.

We all know how much Dad would love that.

Jess

Nov. 22
Dear Rachel,

What was I supposed to do? The last thing we needed was a home for the holidays visit from Jess.

The boot had three one-hundred-dollar bills in it. I took out one of them and mailed it to her.

A hundred dollars is a small price to pay to keep Jess from the door.

Abby

Tim: Hi Abby.

Abby: Oh, hi Tim.

Tim: See, I promised you I'd go first.

Abby: I'm glad you remembered.

Tim: So, you excited about Thanksgiving?

Abby: Thanksgiving isn't an easy time in my family. My brother Johnny died Thanksgiving weekend, and Dad relives it every year.

Tim: That must be hard.

Abby: After a while you get used to soggy stuffing.

Tim: Just out of curiosity, does your father believe in life everlasting?

Abby: I'm not sure. Mom spouts about heaven sometimes but Dad never talks about it.

Tim: My dog died once.

Abby: That's better than twice.

Tim: When my dog died, I knew he'd gone to heaven. I resisted getting a puppy because I was sure Spot would be jealous.

Abby: Maybe that's why I ended up being a girl. To keep Johnny from being jealous.

Tim: When the holidays are over, maybe we could get married.

Abby: Sounds good. Give me a call during halftime of the second game, and I'll see how things are going.

The Most Important Event in My Life
by Abigail Talbott

When I was eleven years old, I was taken for the first time to the grave site of my brother Johnny.

Up until then, I wasn't supposed to know there had been a Johnny. I'd always wondered why Thanksgiving was so hard in my home, but nobody had ever bothered to explain it to me (and I, of course, had never asked).

Johnny had died on the Friday after Thanksgiving, but since Thanksgiving is a floating sort of a holiday, the anniversary date of his death didn't always land on Thanksgiving weekend. It turned out that my parents went to his grave site every year on the anniversary date, and when it fell during Thanksgiving, if we were home (and frequently we weren't, a lot of times we were sent to my grandparents for Thanksgiving), my parents would take Jess with them, and leave Jocelyn to baby-sit me.

I used to wonder where Dad and Mom and Jess had gone, but Jocelyn always had an explanation. Jess had a doctor's appointment, or a session with a therapist or her principal, or even they'd gone shopping for presents for me, and Jess had known exactly what it was I wanted (that intrigued me, since I never knew exactly what it was I wanted).

But on my eleventh birthday, Jess, who was being punished by my parents for having gotten drunk and setting the curtains on fire the night before, slipped out of her room and into mine and told me all about Johnny. It was about time I knew, she said, and of course she was right. Jess tends to be right about a lot of those things, which is one reason why my father hates her so.

Hearing about Johnny was kind of like hearing about sex. At first you don't believe it, but then it makes all the pieces fit together. I ran out of my room, sobbing, confronting my mother (my birthday was on a Saturday that year; otherwise she never would have been home).

Mom cried too, which really scared me. Jocelyn

53

had just started college, so she wasn't home, and I didn't know what to do about Mom crying. Jocelyn would have known, but not me.

After a while, she calmed down, and she told me the whole story of Johnny and the meningitis and how he'd gone to live with Baby Jesus.

Then of course Mom lied, which is one of her best things. Jess had been quite explicit about how it was I came into being, so naturally I asked if it was true, had Johnny lived would she and Dad have bothered having one more kid.

Of course we would have, Mom said. It was funny. Ordinarily Mom and Jess look a lot alike, but at that moment, they bore no resemblance to each other. By age eleven, I knew a lie when I heard one. I really would have preferred the truth. It was a good day for truth, my eleventh birthday. Jess knew that.

Johnny's anniversary date fell on Thanksgiving day that year. Jocelyn came home from college, and for the first time she and I went with Mom and Dad to the grave site. Jess was supposed to go too, but she made a point of getting up early and drinking herself into a stupor, so she got left at home.

I'd been to cemeteries before, when my grandparents had died, but this was different. No funeral, for one thing, and for another Mom drove. We went in the station wagon. Dad has two cars, one all five of us can fit in and a sports car he drives to work, so it was unusual for Mom to be doing the driving.

But I understood why once we got there. Johnny's tombstone had angels on it, his name and birthdate as well as the date of his death, and "Suffer the little children to come unto me" carved on it. Mom had thirteen white roses (one for each year since his death), which she put down on the grave, and that was when Dad started crying.

There was no stopping him once he started. Mom didn't even try. Neither did Jocelyn, which surprised me more. Dad wept. It was like he stored up his tears for a year, and now he could let them loose.

I wanted more than anything else in my entire life to be out of there. I wanted to have nothing to do with these people, this sobbing man and stolid woman. Even Jocelyn, whose very presence had gotten me through eleven complicated years, was alien and horrifying to me. She cried too, just a little, and I couldn't tell whether she was doing it for Dad (to show solidarity) and Mom (who seemed incapable of crying), or because she actually missed Johnny, whom she had once known.

I envied Jess then, Jess who knew enough to get drunk, Jess who knew enough to refuse to be loved by our parents. I envied Johnny, who had been loved so much by our father that in thirteen years he hadn't been forgotten. Dad could barely remember me from one day to the next.

I envied families that didn't have this ritual of the roses, that spent Thanksgiving weekend arguing over drumsticks and wings. I envied families that had died all together in fires and crashes. I stood there and willed myself to sink into the ground, to become one with Johnny's long-dead body, but of course I remained standing, watching, envying.

Jocelyn and Mom supported Dad as we walked back to the station wagon. He sat in the back with me, and Jocelyn sat up front with Mom. Jocelyn offered to drive, but Mom said that wouldn't be necessary. Those were her exact words: "That won't be necessary."

We actually had Thanksgiving dinner that day, turkey and all. Jess was gone when we got home, and she didn't get back until Saturday, so we had supper without her. She didn't miss much. The turkey was dry and the stuffing was tasteless and only Jocelyn spoke, and she didn't say much.

Jess has never gone with us, not since I started going. The next year, she had already run away, and the one or two Thanksgivings she's spent at home since then, she's been in no shape to join us. Jocelyn goes, and every year she offers to drive and every year Mom says it won't be necessary.

I wonder where Mom stores away her tears and if Dad keeps his in the toes of his boots.

Nov. 27
Dear Rachel,

No, no, no, no, no, no, no.

Abby

November 28
Dear Abby,

Did you know when you were born, I cried? The whole business made me so angry, first Johnny dying (I'd really liked having a baby brother) and then Mom announcing there was going to be a new baby in the house and then there you were. I wanted another boy, and I knew Dad did too, and even Jess muttered something about how it wasn't fair (of course, she wouldn't have been any happier if it had been a boy).

But now I can't imagine life without you. There's no one

else I could have talked to the way I talked with you. And everything you told me was right. How did you get to be so smart so young?

You were right to tell me to stick it through until the end of the school year, but unfortunately I still don't think I'm strong enough to make it. But I think I can endure it until the end of the semester, so I won't tell Dad I'm going to quit until then.

I also know you were right when you said it would be cruel of me to tell Dad over Thanksgiving. I should have realized that myself, but I've been so involved with my own misery, I couldn't even think what it would do to him. If Johnny had lived, Dad wouldn't be nearly so involved with my life as he is, but he didn't, and a firstborn just has to do when there isn't a son to cherish.

I hate medical school so much, Abby. I've thought a lot about your question—would I hate being a doctor if I made it through, and I still don't know the answer. But I do know I can never make it through.

I used to tell myself I was going to be a doctor for Dad and Granddad and Great-granddad, but mostly for Johnny, who I knew would have been a doctor if he'd only had the chance. I never once told myself I was going to be a doctor for me, because I found the work interesting or challenging or rewarding or even remunerative.

What I have promised myself is if I do make it through the semester, next semester I'm not going to do anything. I can't move home, I couldn't bear facing Dad every day, but I'll find someplace else to stay and I won't do a thing. I have some money from Granddad's trust, and I'll use it to rent a room somewhere and buy myself enough food to get by.

After I've had six months to think and decide, I'll know what I want to do, and then I'll do it. Maybe I'll go to grad school and get a degree in something I really care about.

Or maybe I'll get a job. I don't think I'll turn into Jess, but at this point, I almost don't care.

I'm sorry you're the one I confide in. I wish there were someone else, but you know how it is with us. We always turn everything in on ourselves. For all those years of my alleged great popularity in school, I never had a real friend I could talk to. I always suspected that if I had, if there was someone I really could talk to, I wouldn't be popular anymore.

Love me, Abby. Love me anyway.

Jocelyn

Dec. 1
Dear Rachel,

Jocelyn's semester ends on December 23. I think about Christmas, how she's going to come home and tell Dad about her change in plans, and my stomach clenches, and I feel nothing but panic.

As long as Jocelyn was there, being good, being perfect, then I didn't have to be. Sure I had to work hard anyway, had to pretend like I cared, like schoolwork mattered, but I knew it was all an act, and so did Dad. He's never thought of me as smart, as someone who could possibly make anything of her life. Sure, I'm no Jess, but in his eyes I'm the princess of mediocrity.

But if Jocelyn quits, if she declares to the world and Dad that she's human after all, what will it do to us? Will Jess suddenly emerge as the dark horse, reforming herself, completing high school and college in the blink of an eye?

Or will everything collapse? Mom's cozy world of lies suddenly dissolve, Dad realize everything in his life, everything, is a failure, and he along with it.

And what of me? Will Dad be forced to notice me now,

and if he does, do I become perfect Jocelyn or monster Jess? Will he expect me to talk to him? I have nothing to say. How can I speak to a man I've never spoken to before?

Jocelyn cannot do this to us. She can't suddenly decide to be imperfect. How dare she choose to be human?

Abby

Abby: Tell me a story, Tim.

Tim: What happened to the Hi Tim, Oh, hi Abby part of our conversation?

Abby: I don't have much time. I need to hear a story.

Tim: What kind of story?

Abby: If I knew that, do you think I'd be asking you?

Tim: Okay. Once upon a time . . .

Abby: Wait a second. Is this a story with a happy ending?

Tim: If that's what you want.

Abby: I do. I want a happy ending.

Tim: Once upon a time there was a princess named Abby. Like all princesses, Abby lived in a castle with a wicked stepmother.

Abby: No.

Tim: What? The castle or the stepmother?

Abby: I don't want anybody wicked in my story.

Tim: It's not going to be a great fairy tale without somebody wicked hanging around. Snow White without the queen, Cinderella without the stepsisters, what are they?

Abby: Tell me a story where everybody's happy, so you can't tell the end from the beginning.

Tim: Once upon a time there was a little boy named Johnny and he stayed on earth for two happy years and then the angels called him and he went to live with Jesus. Happy beginning, happy ending. Satisfied?

Abby: That's it, isn't it. The happy ending.

59

Tim: That's not for me to say.

Abby: But if you don't, who will?

Tim: You know, I used to just be a boy sitting next to you in history class. You didn't make demands on me then, making me tell you stories. You were happy if I just asked to look at your notes.

Abby: Are you happy, Tim?

Tim: Sometimes I think I liked it better when I existed. But except for that, I'm happy.

Abby: What does not existing feel like?

Tim: Ask Johnny.

12/6
Abby—

I don't know if Mom got around to telling you I'm in jail. I used my one phone call to call her at work, see if I could convince her to come up with bail (only five hundred, no more than a boot's worth), but she said she thought not. "I think not," she said. Actually she said "You got yourself into this, you get yourself out," but "I think not" has a nicer, more literary ring to it.

The reason I'm in jail has to do with a little misunderstanding at a local convenience store, which I would describe to you, except my lawyer (supplied by you, the average American taxpayer) says I should keep my mouth shut. Definitely a challenge for me.

I can't say I'm thrilled with life in jail. I miss all the things that got me here in the first place, bad company, bad habits. But I haven't lost hope. Lots of people find God in jail, or at least career alternatives. Maybe I'll learn how to be a safecracker or a cat burglar.

One nice thing about this place, they let you write letters (this may change once I plead guilty to whatever lesser charge they cook up for me). I've already written three

60

times to Jocelyn (making a point of putting my return address in large letters on the front and back of the envelopes), and now I'm writing to you. I wrote to Dad once too, at the hospital, but I know he won't answer.

I guess what I'm trying to say is I know you don't like to write to me, and I can't say as I blame you, mostly all I've ever asked you for is money, and frankly, I wouldn't mind if you got some to me right now, but sometimes here I actually get scared (no, that isn't fair, I'm scared all the time Abby, always have been, can't remember a time when I wasn't), sometimes here I think about my future and it occurs to me I might not die young, I might live to be eighty, through some hideous twist of fate, and what will I be like in my thirties and forties? Will I still crave drugs when I'm fifty?

When I was out, I was busy all the time, drugs are very time-consuming, finding them, taking them, paying for them, but in here all there is is time, and my brain isn't dead yet, no matter how hard I've tried to kill it, and I don't think about my past mistakes, hell I like my past mistakes, I feel cozy with them, comfy, at home, but the future ones scare me Abby, all those mistakes just waiting to be born.

Have you ever felt a pimple right before it emerges? It's there, under the skin, waiting to come out, but when you rub the spot, you feel nothing. That's how I feel now, like my whole skin is about to erupt, but on the surface, there's nothing.

Abby, write to me. I have no one. Dad threw me away a long time ago, and Mom's shed her last tear over me, and Jocelyn thinks of me as an embarrassment, if she thinks of me at all. Send me a letter, Abby. Fill it with lies. I don't want the truth. Nobody in our family does. Nobody outside our family does either.

Jess

61

December 7
Dear Abby,

Just a note to let you know I've been studying hard for my exams, and it's almost not painful, because every day I feel myself closer to leaving, closer to being honest with Dad and Mom and myself.

I've told my two closest friends here of my plan to leave, and I'm the envy of both of them!

See you in a couple of weeks.

Love,
Jocelyn

Abby: All right. I'll tell you a story.

Tim: What makes you think I want to hear one?

Abby: Once upon a time there was a girl with two sisters, and one sister was good and the other was bad.

Tim: What about the girl? What was she like?

Abby: Nobody knew because nobody saw her.

Tim: Did she like that? Not being seen?

Abby: At first she thought she wanted to be good, but then it turned out being good wasn't all it was cracked up to be. Then she thought she'd like to be bad, but that was so much work, more than being good, a real commitment of time and energy, and she didn't have the time because she had to write essays all the time, and she didn't have the energy because she had no energy, she used what energy she had to keep from being seen.

Tim: And what if somebody saw her? What would have happened then?

Abby: She was too scared to find out.

Dec. 9
Dear Rachel,

What am I supposed to do? Do I write to Jess? Do I make social chitchat with my jailbird sister?

And what about Jocelyn? How can she be so happy? How can she just stop caring?

I wonder how Dad's patients feel when they've been cut open, and Dad, and all the other doctors and nurses, are poking around inside their bodies. Fingers touching hearts and lungs and stomachs, squeezing life into them, cutting off the dead parts.

I don't know what to do. I think I'll make out another will.

Abby

LAST WILL AND TESTAMENT

I, Abigail Leigh Talbott, leave everything I have or have ever had or ever dreamed of having to the Jessica Michelle Talbott Legal Defense Fund.

Except for my teddy bears. Those I leave to science, so they can cut them up and try to find their hearts.

The Most Important Event in My Life
by Abigail Talbott

My parents don't know this, but once I went to Johnny's grave site without telling them.

I went with Jess. It was her idea. She said she was going to borrow Dad's car (the family model, not the sports car, which is the one she would have preferred to take, but Dad had used it to drive to the hospital) and take a hop over to the cemetery, did I care to join her?

Jess never asked me to do things with her. Jocelyn did, the way you'd take along a pet dog, but Jess hardly knew I was alive, noticing me only when she wanted to hurt me.

But this time I figured that wasn't her motive, so I said yes. It was a treat to get into the car without Mom or Dad to chauffeur me. Jess didn't have a driver's license, but I knew she knew how to drive (twice she'd been caught stealing the sports car, and once she was nearly twenty miles away before they caught up with her).

Jess, bless her, asked me if I wanted to drive, but I said no. I was eleven and thought it was a very big thing to be in this car with my sister who was treating me as an equal. I thought, someday I'll be a teenager, the same as Jess, and I'll steal cars and get drunk and do all kinds of things I barely know the names of now.

"I like to visit Johnny," Jess said. "I do it lots when Mom and Dad don't know."

Since I had only officially learned about Johnny four months before, this was news to me.

While we drove the two miles to the cemetery, Jess told me all about Johnny. At first she'd been excited to have a baby brother, but then she'd realized Mommy and Daddy didn't love her anymore. They spent all their time with Johnny. "Even Jocelyn was jealous," Jess said. "She'd deny it now, but I remember. Before then Jocelyn could do no wrong, but once Johnny was around, she suddenly became human. It didn't last long, just those two years, but I really liked Jocelyn then. We did all kinds of bad things together, breaking stuff, making messes, and the more bad stuff we did, the more Mom and Dad loved Johnny. It drove Jocelyn crazy."

There was no point asking Jess if it drove her crazy too, since Jess was already crazy, always had been. A crazy Jocelyn was a dizzying concept though, and I giggled at the very thought of it. Jess laughed too. That may have been the only time Jess and I ever laughed together.

The cemetery had a parking lot, and Jess pulled the car into a space. We got out, and she knew where to walk. I'd been there once before, at Thanksgiving, but there were a lot of graves and it helped to know the way.

It was one of those beautiful January days when the air is crisp and cold, and the sun offers just enough warmth to remind you spring will someday return. There was ice on the ground, and Jess held on to me, for the sake of her balance or mine I couldn't be sure of.

Johnny's tombstone was carved out of white marble. It looked clean and pure against the blue sky.

Jess stared at the tombstone for a moment, and then spat at it. She wasn't very good at spitting, and had to do it two or three times before there was any spittle worth mentioning.

"Do something," she said to me.

"What?" I asked.

"Pee on his grave," she suggested.

"I will not," I said. I was eleven years old and not about to go to the bathroom in public. Especially not in January.

"Who do you love better, him or me?" Jess asked.

This was hard to answer. I'd never met Johnny, except for once when he'd floated into my bedroom to say hello, but in my family, that was something of a selling point. Jess I'd known every day of my life, and I'd long since stopped thinking of her in terms of love. But she had invited me to join her, which was more than Johnny had ever done, although he had kind of suggested that Jesus had a space just waiting for me in heaven.

"I want to go home," I said.

Jess glared at me.

"I'm cold," I said, which wasn't really true. "Take me home."

"Do you love Mom and Dad?" Jess asked.

I began to cry.

Jess shook her head.

"If we were in a boat, Mom and Dad and me, and the boat fell over and we were all drowning and you could only save one of us, which one of us would you save?" Jess asked.

In spite of myself, I found the question interesting. I knew right away I wouldn't rescue Jess, who I no longer liked, even if she had invited me. If I saved Mom, then she'd be a widow, no Dad, and I had no idea what that would be like. Mom worked almost as hard as Dad did, and lots of times she had to stay late at the office or go out on weekends. If Dad was dead, would Mom stay home more often, or would she just move to the office, and I'd see even less of her?

But what if I saved Dad? If I did, he'd be sure to love me. I pictured Dad saying, "I love you Abby, because you saved my life," and I felt warm all over.

"I'd save Dad," I told Jess.

That wasn't the right answer. Jess got so mad she pushed me onto the ground. She scared me, and I thought she'd kick me or beat me up.

"Okay, I'll save you," I said.

"Too late," Jess said. "Now you have to walk home."

"No," I said, but it didn't help. Jess ran away from me, leaving me alone on the ground by Johnny's grave. I thought about chasing after her, but I was too scared, so I stayed where I was until in the distance I could hear her start Dad's car and drive off.

I got up, brushed myself off, and wished Johnny would float back into my life to show me the way out. But that's how it is with dead brothers. You can never count on them showing up when you need them.

It was starting to get dark, and I grew more and more fearful that I'd get lost in the cemetery, never find my way out, die surrounded by death. I was crying hard then, and my body hurt from falling on the hard ground.

What happened then? you ask. Did young Abby get lost and die as she so feared? Or was there a miracle, a path illuminated by the heavens to lead her back home?

Neither, really. I walked around a while, rubbing my nose against my winter coat, and eventually I found the road that led the way out, and once I was back on the street, I knew my way home. When I got there, Dad's car was there, but Jess was gone. Dad was still at the hospital, and Mom didn't come home until after I'd gone to bed.

I was glad to be alone in the house. I made something for supper, turned on the TV, and spent the rest of the evening doing my homework and thinking about drowning.

LAST WILL AND TESTAMENT

I, Abigail Leigh Talbott, aged sixteen and three months, leave the following things to the following people.

To my sister Jocelyn, I leave all my money. She can use it to find herself.

To my sister Jessica, I leave my teddy bears, even though when I was little, she tore one of them to shreds and set another one of them on fire.

To Tim Flannery, who sits next to me in history class, I leave my notes, my diaries, my letters, so that he might know me in death as he never has in life.

To my mother, I leave my bed, which was her choice anyway, bought for a daughter she could only imagine.

To my father

Dec. 13
Dear Rachel,

The closer it gets to Jocelyn's return home, the more frightened I become. If I could only predict what Dad will do, then I wouldn't be so scared. But I can't even imagine. I have never known Dad when he wasn't trying to protect Jocelyn from Jess and Mom and me.

I remember once toward the end of Jocelyn's junior year, Mom wanted to take her shopping, to buy her a dress for the senior prom (she was going with the president of the senior class), and Dad got furious when Mom suggested it. Jocelyn had exams to study for, a big test in chemistry two days away, and another in history at the end of the week. Dad always knew Jocelyn's test schedule, much the way he knows his surgical schedule. Mom, of course, gave way immediately. She made arrangements instead with the local prom-dress shop to take three dresses home for Jocelyn to examine. Jocelyn picked one, a pale rose silk that made her look beautiful, like a queen. That's what Dad said. I wasn't sure I liked the dress at all. It made Jocelyn look like a stranger to me.

The day before the prom, Jocelyn invited Jess and me into her room and asked Jess if she'd like to try the dress on. This was an act of immense kindness on her part, and one that Jess responded to with excitement and gratitude. Pale rose turned out not to be Jess's color, but even so she looked like a different person in that dress, like someone . . . I don't know. Like someone with hope.

Jocelyn offered to wear the same dress to her senior prom, but Dad said no, a new dress was required for the occasion, and since it was second semester senior year, there was plenty of time for Jocelyn to actually shop for one. The dress she bought for herself didn't look anything

69

like her previous year's model. It was ivory colored and beaded and she looked less like a queen and more like a flapper. She gave the dress to Jess once the prom was over, and Jess used to take it out of its garment bag and stare at it. Eventually she took scissors to it and shredded it. I don't know where the rose dress is anymore.

I know what Dad demands of me, how hard he makes me work to keep me from mediocrity, but it's nothing compared to what he demands of Jocelyn. The difference is Jocelyn never seemed to mind. She welcomed the challenge, knew it for what it was, Dad's way of loving her. And the way she succeeded was her way of loving him.

Now what? Will Dad think Jocelyn no longer loves him? Does she? Did she ever? Jess is safely out of it, unavailable for last-minute distractions, breaking and entering, stealing money, making scenes. Mom won't know what to do. She never does. She's never home to find out.

And what happens to me if Dad decides Jocelyn is no longer worthy of his love? Does that mean he'll decide to love me? I don't think I could stand it if he did. It's hard enough now, trying to get 97s. I am not an A-plus person; it will kill me if he makes me turn into one.

Sometimes I think about Johnny, the way he was when I met him, and how wise he seemed, and I think he must have always been that way, and that was why he died. He knew what his life would have been like, and he eagerly caught meningitis, embracing his death.

Abby

Dec. 18
Dear Jess,

Do you remember the time

Dec. 18
Dear Jocelyn,

Are you a fool? Do you have any idea what it will do to
us, what it will do to me, if you go ahead with your plan?
You say all the time that you love me, but you don't know
what love is. You think love is something you have due
you, that naturally people will love you, and you don't
care what you do to anybody else just as long as you're
happy.

Why should you be happy all the time? Nobody else is.
I never thought you would betray me, Jocelyn. Ignore me,
sure, condescend to me, exploit me, even

Abby: Tim? Are you there?

Tim: What kind of question is that?

Abby: I don't know anything anymore.

Tim: You're lying, Abby. You know where Jess is, right
where she belongs. You know where your father is, actually doing good in the one way he knows how. You know
where your mother is, or at least you can make an edu-
cated guess. You know where Jocelyn is, being perfect
until the last possible moment. You know where Johnny
is. You know that best of all.

Abby: Where am I?

Tim: Where do you want to be?

Abby: Asleep.

Tim: That's easy enough to arrange.

Abby: If I go to sleep, will you come with me?

71

Tim: You know I will.

Abby: What do I have to do before I can sleep?

Tim: You know exactly what you have to do. The only question is, will you do it?

Abby: Don't leave me, Tim.

Tim: I couldn't, even if I wanted to.

Dec. 19
Dear Rachel,

You think sometimes you don't know the answers, and then you find you recognize the test, you've seen it before, and your pen races over the page, filling in the blanks, turning multiple choices into single answers, separating the trues from the falses.

The funny thing about the future is you can never be quite sure how it's going to turn out, but I'm tired of worrying about it, tired of figuring out where am I going to fit in, how much change will change me.

Let them all grade my paper. For once I don't care if I pass or fail.

Abby

LAST WILL AND TESTAMENT

I, Abigail Leigh Talbott, aged sixteen and three months, do hereby leave all my worldly goods to my brother John now dead these many years.

If he doesn't show up to claim them, I want everything divided equally between my two sisters, Jocelyn and Jessica, both flawed and disappointing people.

72

To my parents, I leave questions, recriminations, and guilt. They are no strangers to these things, and probably wouldn't be comfortable without them.

Abigail Leigh Talbott

To whom It May Concern:

I don't know if I'm going to die or not. I'm a newcomer to this game, and there may be tricks I have to learn, or maybe I'll be lucky, and get it right the first time.

I really hate being alive.

abby

Part | 2

Abby: Johnny, is that you?

Tim: It's just me, Abby. I was wondering if I could borrow your notes.

12/20

Abby—

I just got a call from Jocelyn telling me what you did. Congratulations! I thought a lot over the years about trying to kill myself, but I was afraid I'd succeed, and I'd hate giving Mom and Dad the satisfaction.

I'm glad you didn't make it all the way to Johnny Land. I'd miss you if you were gone (bet you never thought you'd hear those words from me!).

I can't say as I blame you for exploring Mom's mystery-drug supply. She sure does collect some interesting sedatives. I used to dabble with them myself. Vodka chasers really do make the meal, don't they?

Okay. Enough sympathy. Here are the words of wisdom from somebody who's been there. First of all, stop. Once is fun; twice is boring; three times is dangerous. I am a major-league fuckup, have been since birth. You're not, never have been, never should be. Besides, this family is only big enough for one total disaster, and I have first dibs.

Second (I'll tell you, it's amazing what a month away from drugs does to my brain. I can practically feel the gray cells coming back to life. I am not pleased about it), Mom and Dad are sure to offer you the therapy route. Poor little Abby, maybe we can save her yet. God knows they tried enough with me. I say take them up on it. For starters, it costs a lot of money, all of which they'll have to pay. And you never talk to anyone. You might not think I noticed that, but I have. I certainly noticed that you haven't written to me, except for that once you slipped me a hundred to keep me from a family reunion. Even then it came folded up in a blank piece of paper. If I were more sensitive, I might have been offended.

So let Mom and Dad find someone for you to talk to, and then you can complain to him at great expense. It isn't like they're shelling out anything for my legal defense.

Jess

P.S. Abby, if I can make it to twenty-one, there's no reason why you can't too.
P.P.S. Merry Christmas!

Dec. 22
Dear Rachel,

All right, it was stupid of me. The more I think about it, the more stupid I know it was. And I can't even claim it was a spontaneous act. I'd been thinking about it for months. You don't work on last wills and testaments without a reason.

It was just as I was losing consciousness that I first began to wonder why the hell I was doing it. What was so bad? So what if Jocelyn dropped out of medical school? What was the big deal? I'd spent sixteen adequate years being alone. Despair shouldn't equal death.

There's nothing like being rational a moment too late.

The funny thing was, after I passed out, I thought I saw Johnny again, the way he looked that one time he came to visit. I reached out for him, I remember the sensation of stretching my arm out, but he floated away before I could grab him. He didn't seem mad or anything, not even disappointed, just distant and uncaring (sound like anyone you know?). I called out to him (something I've never done with Dad), but he turned out to be Tim, asking if he could borrow my notes. Which, oddly enough, I didn't have with me on my road to oblivion.

That Tim. What a kidder.

So now I'm alive, and Jocelyn will be home tomorrow to God knows what, and Mom and Dad keep looking at me funny, and I'm getting letters of sisterly advice from Jess.

Other than that, things are great.

Abby

Abby: Hi Tim.

Tim: Oh, hi Abby. It's nice to see you alive.

Abby: At school today, did you think to say anything to me? Anything real I mean. You must have known what I tried. I may not be noticeable at home, but a suicide attempt is always good for a little talk in the cafeteria.

Tim: That's not fair. You know perfectly well there are two Tims, the one you carry on these conversations with in the privacy of your bedroom, and the real one, the one who hardly knows you're alive (except when it comes to borrowing notes). I can't be responsible for the real Tim, and I certainly don't know what goes on in his mind. You want to know, you ask him yourself.

Abby: Don't I get any sympathy from you?

Tim: Why should I be different from anybody else you know? I haven't noticed your parents pulling out the violins and roses.

Abby: Jocelyn will care. She let Jess know, after all.

Tim: Fine. Tell Jocelyn to ask the real Tim what he thinks about your little trip.

Abby: I wish I had a friend.

Tim: I could be wrong, but I don't think suicide attempts are real good icebreakers.

Dec. 23
Dear Rachel,

Jocelyn came home this evening with all her bags and boxes. Lucky for me, Dad was in surgery, and Mom wasn't home yet either.

That gave Jocelyn just the opportunity she was looking for to rip into me, which she did. God, I used to think it was bad when Dad gave me one of his mediocrity speeches, but that was nothing compared to what I felt while Jocelyn gave me a piece of her mind. Of course I love Jocelyn, which could make a difference.

How dare I try to kill myself? How dare I presume that my problems were worthy of such a drastic step? I was spoiled, self-centered, and selfish, and could give Jess a lesson or two in stupidity.

Of course I cried, and then Jocelyn hugged me, but then she said she had no intention of changing her plans just because of my little stunt (if I'd succeeded, would it have been my big stunt?), and she never wanted me to think I had any power over her major life decisions.

I never thought I had any power over anything, and nothing in the past week's changed my mind about that.

So then we got chatty, and she asked me what having my stomach pumped felt like (I guess now that she's giving up medicine, she regrets never having the chance to do it to someone), and what had Mom and Dad said about it, etc. I told her the truth, that they hadn't said much of anything, and Jocelyn looked very disapproving. I guess she feels they should have given me the speech about my little stunt, instead of leaving it all up to her.

I thanked her for telling Jess, and she said she'd only done it to show Jess how much was her fault, which was very Jocelyn, and somewhat unfair. It wasn't Jess who had decided to drop out of medical school and ruin everything.

80

Of course I didn't tell Jocelyn that. I just said that I'd gotten a letter from Jess, and she didn't like what I'd done either, and Jocelyn pursed her lips (she really did) and said jail was probably the best thing that ever happened to Jess, and she only hoped Jess ended up in one for a couple of years, so she'd have a chance to straighten herself out.

I am related to maniacs without exception.

Jocelyn told me I should get into therapy, and I told her Jess seemed to think so too, but I didn't see what good it would do me, and I probably wouldn't try killing myself again, at least not until I was out of the house (at which point, why kid ourselves, why will I need to?), but Jocelyn said suicide attempts don't just come from nowhere, and it would be better for me to get straightened out when I was sixteen than to brush everything under the carpet and really go crazy in a year or two.

I think I preferred the self-deluding, we're-such-a-great-happy-family Jocelyn.

I almost asked her if it bothered her that neither of her parents thought it was important enough to be home when she got there, but I didn't. It wasn't like I was looking forward to the confrontation (which Jocelyn informs me she has scheduled for tomorrow, so they'll be over the shock by Christmas. Talk about self-deluding). Besides, once we finished with the lectures, it was nice having her back. Not that I can talk to her, but I can not talk to her better than anybody else in the family (which means in the world).

Abby

Abby: Hi Tim.

Tim: Oh, hi Abby.

Abby: I just thought you should know that someday I'm going to stop talking to you like this. I'm going to talk to the real Tim instead, just walk right up to him and say Hi Tim, the way I say it to you, only he'll talk back to me about real stuff. Unlike certain other Tims I could name.

Tim: You think that's a threat? Go, do it.

Abby: Hasn't it occurred to you, you won't exist once I stop writing these little dialogues?

Tim: Let me tell you something. You think you invented me, but you didn't. You just borrowed my spirit for as long as you needed it, and when you don't anymore, I'll float away and go someplace else, make a home for myself in someone else's imagination. She won't call me Tim, but I'll still be me. I'm going to last a lot longer than you ever will, Abigail Leigh Talbott.

Abby: You can do that? Just float?

Tim: Only humans sink, Abby. Spirits know how to float.

The Most Important Event in My Life
by Abigail Talbott

I know what you think I'm going to write, that my extremely recent suicide attempt was the most important event in my life, and I'm sure if I'd died, it would have been the most important event, even more important than the time Johnny came calling (although if I'd succeeded, I know I would have spent a lot of time with him, swapping gossip and recipes and tips on floating).

You want to know, don't you, anonymous reader of student applications, what it felt like, why I did it, how did people react. You want to see the action, Mom walking in on me (who would have thought she'd pick that day to come home from work at 5:30), seeing my body lying on the family room floor, one arm stretched out (I was reaching for Johnny), the hurried phone call to 911, the ambulance, the emergency room (none of which I remember of course), the stomach pumping, the woozy sense of coming back to life, the hideous expression of embarrassment and distaste on Dad's face when he saw me in his precious hospital, his home away from work. You want me to tell you the exact length of time Mom felt concern about me, as though you could put a stopwatch to emotions (she drove me home the next morning from the hospital, setting a personal best of seventeen hours, if you include the ones she slept through). You want to know if I feel remorse, if I've come to my senses, if it's a reasonable investment on your part, welcoming me into your hallowed halls, or will I just find myself another pill collection, a new bottle of liquor, and end up on some dormitory floor for you to mop up.

Well I hate to disappoint you, but I have no intention of writing about any of that. Maybe some other time when I can't quite see how Dad looked, when I can no longer remember how quiet the house was after Mom dropped me off on her way to the office. Someday my little suicide attempt will be just that, a little suicide attempt, a childhood anecdote, a detail in my autobiography.

Instead I'm going to write about the most important event in my life, the way Dad is always telling me to, something I can use in my efforts (already doomed to failure) to get into a decent college. I'm going to tell you about Jocelyn instead, the heroine of this story, about one of the many times she was perfect, so you'll know why I love her.

I was ten, and had managed to be ten mostly

by being invisible. I'd learned a few years before that no one at home could really see me, and there didn't seem much point in showing up at school either. The easiest way of being invisible in the outside world was by doing whatever I was told to do, no questions, no complaints, and since the only thing I ever did at home was schoolwork, I had great grades and my teachers all loved me. I was well behaved. They said so every time on my report card. Maybe I should be a little more outgoing ("Abby doesn't seem to have many friends"), but really I was a lovely, quiet, old-fashioned child. That's probably why Mom insisted on the brass bed.

But in fifth grade, I had one of those go-getter teachers, only at it for a year or two, determined to make the rowdy kids quiet, and the quiet kids rowdy. She picked me to star in the class play.

All the other girls, the ones who actually spoke in school, objected, but Ms. Green insisted. I had the best grades, she said, and the student with the best grades deserved to star in the class play. A whole new approach to casting.

At first I kept it to myself that this particular honor had fallen my way. To be perfectly honest, if there'd been any way at all to keep from letting my family know, I would never have told them. But Jocelyn, all the way up in high school, heard about it, and she made a point of congratulating me one evening when we all five were at the dinner table together. That happened a lot more often those days, the five of us under the same roof. It wasn't until Jocelyn left for college that Mom and Dad began avoiding home. At first I thought it was because they wanted to steer clear of Jess, who had been bad while Jocelyn still lived with us, but got a lot worse once she left, but by the following year, Jess was pretty much gone for good, and Mom and Dad never got around to coming back. Sometimes I think it's me they're avoiding. Sometimes I know it is.

So there we all are, a pretty picture, the American family at the dinner table together, and Jocelyn says, why didn't you tell us Abby, that you were starring in your class play, and so I have to tell them. It's not that big a part, I assure them, and I didn't get it because I have any talent or anything, but I'd never starred before, so they figured it was my turn, and sure I was going to tell them, but I'd forgotten.

Forgotten? Dad said. How could you forget that you're starring in your class play?

Now, now, John, Mom said. I'm sure what Abby means is the part isn't important to her, and that's why she didn't tell us about it.

I nodded, although, of course, the part was desperately important to me, my one chance to shine, to be someone I wasn't, to be a star. I liked the idea of being a star, since sometimes I thought that was what Johnny had turned into after he'd died.

Dad grunted and Jess yawned, and undoubtedly Mom then turned the conversation back to Jocelyn, who was the only one of us who knew how to talk to the others.

The class play was scheduled for Thursday night, as part of an evening's entertainment for young and old alike. Mom had been saying all week long that she and Dad would be there to see me, but I can't say I was surprised (or even disappointed) when it turned out neither of them could make it. There'd been a three-car pileup, with various mangled bodies that needed Dad to put them back together, to serve as his excuse, and Mom had forgotten that her brief had to be in court by Friday, 9 A.M., so she was going to have to work all night at the office to get it done. I wasn't even surprised (or disappointed) that neither of them told me directly, instead conveying the information through Jocelyn (even that isn't accurate— Mom called Jocelyn to say she couldn't make it, then told Jocelyn to call Dad and remind him, but when Jocelyn did, she was told about the car crash instead). Jocelyn told me not to worry, she would personally drive me to school, and she and Jess would attend the class play and cheer enough for all of them.

I thanked her. I was a very polite ten-year-old.

Jess had a gift even then. First she denounced Mom and Dad for their callous disregard for my feelings, and then while I was in my room getting into my costume (I played Martha Washington, the class play was all about First Ladies), she moseyed her way to the liquor cabinet and got very drunk very fast.

Poor Jocelyn didn't know what to do. It wasn't that she hadn't seen Jess drunk before, but never when she'd have to leave her alone in the house. So she told Jess she had to come with us, which Jess didn't seem to mind. At that point, Jess didn't mind anything. When she was younger, she was a very happy drunk.

The three of us got into Jocelyn's car (given to her for her sixteenth birthday, not that I got one for mine), Jess sitting next to Jocelyn and giggling the entire trip, me in the back, staring out the window, feeling more and more miserable. Not because Mom and Dad wouldn't be there, or even because Jess was drunk and sure to cause a scene. No, the misery had to do with me, and how wrong it was that I'd even think about starring in anything, even something as unimportant as a fifth-grade play.

Some people are born to play Martha Washington. And some of us are not.

Jocelyn pulled into the school parking lot, told Jess to stop giggling, and turned to me with that this'll-be-great smile of hers. You're going to be wonderful, she said. I can't wait to see you onstage.

I can't do it, I said. I can't go on. I can't.

Poor Jocelyn. In the course of an hour, she'd had to deal with Mom, then Dad, a drunken Jess, and now me. Of course you can, she said. You'll be great. Just get out of the car and go backstage, and things will be fine.

No, I said. I can't. I won't. You can't make me.

Jess thought that was extremely funny.

I know you know your lines, Jocelyn said. I've heard you go over them every night for the past week. You look beautiful in your costume, and you're sure to be a big hit.

No, I said.

You have to go on, Jocelyn said. What will we tell Mom and Dad?

Tell them she went on, Jess suggested. They won't care enough to find out the truth.

I knew Jess was right. Not that it mattered.

Jocelyn stared at me, and then she looked at Jess, and I think it all hit her then, how unfair it was that she had to look after not only her shy unhappy youngest sister, but her raucous drunken middle sister as well, that she wasn't my mother, or Jess's, and Mom and Dad had no business treating her as though she was.

Fine, she said. She took off her coat, used it as a curtain, and told me to take off my costume, which I did. She then put her coat around me and ran into the school building, carrying with her all that which made me Martha Washington. When she came back, she said she'd told Ms. Green that I had laryngitis, and Dad had forbidden me to perform, for fear of doing permanent damage to my vocal cords.

Jess thought that was the funniest thing of all.

When we got home, I didn't want to take Jocelyn's coat off. I felt protected in it, warm and sheltered, but Jocelyn was in no mood herself, and she made me. I went to my room, where I stayed, without interruption, for the rest of my life. Mom and Dad continued working, Jocelyn drove to college with a new winter coat, and Jess went off to explore degradation, but I'd found where I belonged and saw no reason ever to stray again.

Abby: Can you hear them?

Tim: Calm down. Don't listen if it bothers you that much.

Abby: How can I not listen? They're screaming at each other.

Tim: Write another essay. Put a pillow over your head. Think about Johnny.

Abby: I want them to stop.

Tim: Then tell them to.

Abby: Oh sure. They're just about to do what I ask them.

Tim: You have a weapon now. Tell them you'll try to kill yourself again if they don't stop screaming.

Abby: Would that work?

Tim: I don't know. But I think it's worth a try.

Dec. 24
Dear Rachel,

I never should have left my room, never, I should know what a mistake that is, to leave my room, to remind them of me, I'm sixteen years old, I've had sixteen years of them, you'd think I'd know by now not to leave my room no matter how bad things are, if the house was burning, I should stay in my room.

They were in the family room, and Dad was shouting at Jocelyn, how dare she just make an announcement like that, throwing away the plans of a lifetime because she was tired, and Jocelyn was shouting back that she wasn't just tired like she hadn't gotten any sleep the night before, she was tired because her entire life she was expected to do things, take on responsibilities that shouldn't have been hers to shoulder, and Mom started shouting then too, saying I suppose you think this is all my fault, and the three of them were such a cozy little triangle of hate that I was sure there was no point in speaking, that they could never hear me. I'd witnessed that scene too many times before with Jess, only now it was Jocelyn, who had lied to Ms. Green for me, and had been just as willing not to lie, but to go to the damn class play and cheer as though she were my parents.

So I screamed Stop it! and when they didn't hear me the first time, I screamed it again STOP IT! and this time they did.

Oh God, Dad said. Now what.

It's not Jocelyn's fault, I said, although I believed every bit as much as he did that it was.

Abby dear, this really doesn't concern you, Mom said. Why don't you go back to your room and watch a little TV.

Just the opening Jocelyn was looking for. How can you say that to her, she demanded. Acting as though she isn't a member of this family. She tried to kill herself a week ago, a week ago, and all you can say to her is why don't you go to your room and watch a little TV? Of course, by then, the only thing I wanted to do was go to my room and watch a little TV.

You have no feelings for her, do you, she said. Jess, at least you hate, there's some emotion there, but Abby doesn't even exist for you. She's just your second try at a son, and when she didn't turn out the way you wanted, you told her to go to her room and watch some TV.

This is not about Abby, Dad said. This is about you, Jocelyn, and why you've decided to throw your life away.

Abby's a symbol, Jocelyn said, for everything that's wrong with this family.

I wanted to be dead then, more than I'd ever wished it, more than when I was writing my wills, more than when I was writing my suicide note, more than when I was downing Mom's pills with Dad's vodka. Only you don't die when you want to. You don't die just from standing in the doorway of the family room hearing the only person you were ever sure loved you using you as a weapon against your parents.

We're dealing with Abby's problems, Mom said (news to me). Right now, we're focusing on yours, Jocelyn.

Jocelyn wasn't satisfied. How are you dealing with them? she asked. Getting her stomach pumped? Giving her a lift home from the hospital, instead of sending a cab to pick her up?

We're looking for a therapist, Mom said. It isn't easy you know. We went through a half dozen of them with Jess, and we want to find someone who can bring a new perspective to Abby's problems.

You'd better find one fast, Jocelyn said. Abby's problems aren't going to go away just because you're conducting a talent search.

The world does not revolve around Abby's problems,

Dad said, and it sounded funny hearing him say my name. He must call me by name sometimes, when he's warning me about my mediocrity, but I couldn't remember ever hearing him say Abby before. The odds are he does, and I just choose to forget. What we're discussing right now is you, and your newly discovered passion for self-destruction.

For self-preservation you mean, Jocelyn said, and I knew they were through talking about me, and I could slip back to my room, and none of them would know I was gone. I lingered for a moment, marveling that Dad could use the exact same tone with Jocelyn that he had perfected on Jess. I can see now that we're all interchangeable in his eyes; the three of us are no more than failed Johnny tries.

I wonder if Jess's jail cell can hold three.

Abby

The Most Important Event in My Life
by Abigail Talbott

When I was six years old, I got sick, at least as sick as I've ever gotten, and for a couple of days, I was sufficiently sick that people actually worried about me. My older brother Johnny, long dead, floated by for a visit, bringing me regards from Jesus, but I was a lot more interested in Santa.

I was well by the time Christmas rolled around, but I remember that Christmas as the happiest one this family has ever had (of course the ones they had with Johnny must have been much better, but I wasn't on earth to witness them). I think everybody's good mood might have been caused (at least in part) by my recent illness and recovery.

We had a tree that year (we had trees until Jocelyn started college, at which point someone decided it wasn't worth the bother), a big beautifully shaped one, almost as pretty as the ones you see on TV, and even when Jess dropped one of the glass balls and it shattered, nobody shouted at her. That was probably the most important event in her life, or certainly the most unusual.

I still believed in Santa Claus, but in that peaceful fading way kids that age have. What I really believed in was presents. I wanted everything that year, dolls and bikes and my own radio and toys I'd seen on commercials for months already. I'd pestered and plagued, especially when I'd been in bed recovering. I might have been only six, but I knew how to take advantage of a situation.

We decorated the tree Christmas Eve, and we sang carols. Jess, then and now, has a beautiful singing voice, so she got the solos. There was a fire in the fireplace, the TV set was off, everybody was sober and happy and warm.

I had a lot of trouble falling asleep that night, concerned that Santa had forgotten about me (he might, after all, have been told I was too sick to want anything that year) and half expecting another visit from Johnny. I heard noises from the rest of the house, but since I was the youngest, and always put to bed first, that wasn't unusual.

Eventually I fell asleep, and when I woke up everything was dark and quiet. I got out of bed and tiptoed to the family room. Neither Dad nor Mom liked being woken by noisy children.

There was the tree, still beautifully decorated, and under it were hundreds of presents, so many I couldn't count them. But the most beautiful present of

92

all was a dollhouse, Victorian in style, with eight rooms and an attic on the inside, a front porch and ginger-bread on the outside. It was perfection, and I stared at it, not daring to touch it, because anything that perfect could only be for Jocelyn.

I tried to convince myself that Jocelyn was too old for dollhouses, that even if it was intended for her, she'd certainly let me touch it, and probably let me play with it, but still I didn't dare go near it. It's funny. If it were one of Jess's things, and I touched it, she would have hit me or twisted my arm. Jess was very big on territoriality. But Jocelyn was nothing like that. Jocelyn was seven years older than me and she thought I was cute. It was safe to touch her things, especially if there was no way she would know that I had. But even so, I kept my distance, looking at the dollhouse, wanting to examine its furnishings, its occupants, but not allowing myself to stand too close to it for fear I'd lose control.

Jess woke up next, and she too was silenced by the beauty of the dollhouse. "I bet it's for you," she said, but I shook my head. "It must be for Jocelyn," I said.

"No," Jess said. "Jocelyn's too old for that stuff. It's for you."

I thought about it for a moment and realized Jess might be right. Mom and Dad would have bought something that perfect only for Jocelyn, but Santa might well have brought it for me. I'd been very care-ful to be good for years, and Johnny had told me that Santa loved me.

But I wasn't about to take any chances. It was exciting enough just being in the same room with the dollhouse and thinking that it might be mine.

Mom and Dad walked into the family room together. They looked different, and I realized it was because they were holding hands. "Merry Christmas," Mom said, and she kissed both of us, Jess first, and then me.

"Like the dollhouse, Abby?" Dad asked.

"It's beautiful," I said. "It's the most beautiful thing I've ever seen." I didn't dare ask who it was for.

"We thought you'd like it," Mom said. Her voice was softer than usual, but I figured that was just to keep from waking Jocelyn.

"Did Santa bring it for me?" I asked, trying to sound cool just in case it really was for Jocelyn.

"Santa!" Dad exploded. "I spent six hours last night assembling that damn thing, and you think Santa Claus brought it to you?"

"Calm down John," my mother said. "Abby, some of these presents are from Santa, but the dollhouse is from your father and me. Merry Christmas, honey."

Only then did I allow myself to examine the dollhouse. The closer I got to it, the more splendid I saw it was. There were doors that opened and tiny curtains on the windows, servants' quarters in the attic, and a little baby in a cradle in one of the upstairs bedrooms.

"Only a surgeon could have assembled that damn thing," Dad said, but he didn't sound scary anymore, more proud, and almost like it was a joke. So I did something I hardly ever did and had certainly never been encouraged to do. I walked over to Dad on my own and kissed him.

"I love you Dad," I said. I wanted to call him Daddy but we weren't allowed.

"I love you too, Abigail," he said, awkwardly hugging me. "Now, what's for breakfast?" he bel-

94

lowed. "A man works up a mighty appetite building houses for his daughter."

Jess laughed. I was terrified.

But Dad and Mom laughed too, and I realized I didn't have to be scared, and I wasn't, not for the entire rest of the day, and I stayed not scared until New Year's Eve, when Mom and Dad went to a party and both got drunk and fought terribly when they got home. It was almost a relief by then to be scared, like welcoming home a lost puppy.

Abby: Tell me about the worst Christmas you ever had.

Tim: Why? Are we playing my life is worse than your life?

Abby: I'd win. Take my word for it.

Tim: Don't forget, I'm a spirit. I've spent Christmas with Tiny Tim, before Scrooge reformed. I can do pathos if that's what you're interested in.

Abby: Only my own, thank you.

Tim: Look at it this way. They're not mad at you.

Abby: That's nothing. They're never mad at me. I try to kill myself, and they're still not mad at me.

Tim: Try killing one of them. That might do it.

Abby: Very funny.

Tim: One of those sharp kitchen knives could do some damage. I bet not even Jess has tried that.

Abby: Stop it.

Tim: You don't have to aim to kill. Go for your father's hands, your mother's face. Do your damage fast while they're sleeping. Catch them by surprise. In less than a minute you could destroy both of them. And what will they do to you? Lock you away someplace with other rich crazed kids? Big deal.

95

Abby: I'm not meant for knives. That's not who I am.

Tim: I hate to point this out to you, but who you are ain't working. Come on. Give it a try. At least think about it, how they'd feel, the blood pouring from their bodies, the way they'd finally hate you, the way they hate Jess, the way they're starting to hate Jocelyn. That's what you want, isn't it? If they hate you, at least they'll acknowledge you're alive.

Abby: You're scaring me.

Tim: Sorry. If you want, I'll go back to borrowing your notes.

Dec. 26
Dear Rachel,

Well I hope someone had a merry Christmas. Around here it was an armed camp, Mom and Dad on one side, Jocelyn on the other, and me in my room, fantasizing about slaughter.

That isn't completely true. At about eleven in the morning, when I realized no matter how hard I wished for it, Santa was not going to bring us peace for the holidays, I started on all the homework I'd been assigned, and I worked straight through the day and did everything I'd been given to do.

This is going to be one long hard vacation.

Abby

12/26
Abby—

I hope you had a great Christmas. It wasn't too bad here, all things considered. Some socially conscious ladies group made us a special Christmas meal, which, given the food

96

we usually get, was a real treat. We sang carols too. I'd forgotten how much I like singing, and I got a lot of compliments ("nice voice for a white girl").

Can't say I missed Christmas with the family very much. Mom and Dad were always pretty good with presents, but they could never really guess what I wanted, and I knew whatever I gave them wouldn't be right.

Once, I must have been eleven since I still cared about that sort of thing, I overheard Dad saying there was a certain book he wanted, and I saved my allowance and bought it for him for Christmas, but when he unwrapped it, he said he already had it, he'd bought himself a copy of it weeks before. Which is why, by twelve, I no longer cared.

None of which is why I wrote, but there is something about the holidays that makes you nostalgic. What I wanted to say was I've been thinking a lot about you, and I still think this therapy idea is the best one, but make sure Mom and Dad don't saddle you with Dr. Howard. I had him when I was about fourteen, and he used to kiss me and other stuff. He said I needed "tangible evidence of affection."

He was the only shrink I had that tried anything with me, so you're probably safe, but I didn't like the idea of him pawing you, so I figured I'd warn you.

Write to me and let me know how things are going. I haven't heard from Jocelyn in a while, and I've kind of been wondering how everybody is.

Jess

Dec. 29
Dear Rachel,

Jocelyn moved out today. She repacked her bags and her boxes, put them in her car, and drove off.

97

Mom and Dad were both at work when she left, and I was in my room and didn't even hear her until she started her car. I ran out to try and stop her, but she'd already driven off.

I'm scared. I am so scared. What are Mom and Dad going to do when they come home and find Jocelyn's gone?

They're going to make me leave my room. I just know it. They're going to make me leave my room and talk to them and I don't know if they're going to mistake me for Jocelyn or Jess, but they won't have anything to say to me, Abby, and I have nothing to say to them, and I can't be perfect, and I can't be bad, and all I can be is nothing, and I don't think they're going to let me be that anymore.

What am I going to do? I can't even talk to Tim anymore; he keeps telling me about kitchen knives, and that makes me think about what it would feel like to cut my wrists, and I can't let myself think about things like that.

I loved my dollhouse. When I was eight I spent a full year trying to will myself to be so small I could move into it. I knew if I did that, Mom and Dad could never find me, even if they bothered to look.

I'd run away if I could, but I wouldn't know what to do once I got wherever I'd end up. Jess at least had the basic skills to be a whore, but I don't know how to do anything except my homework.

I'm going to go to Jocelyn's room. Maybe she left me some instructions.

Abby

December 28
Dear Abby,

I'm sorry to do this to you, just leave without any notice, but the way things are going here, I can't bear to stay a minute longer.

When I was younger, and still lived at home, I'd watch what Mom and Dad did to Jess, but no matter how hard they were on her, I knew she deserved it. She might not have started out bad, but certainly by the time Johnny was born, she was determined to cause trouble. She tried to kill Johnny, you know. I saw her put the pillow over his mouth, and if I hadn't pushed her away, I think she would have succeeded. After that, I didn't care what Mom and Dad did to her.

But God, now that I've had a taste of their medicine, I'm starting to sympathize with Jess, starting to feel how she must have felt, and it terrifies me. I can't have Mom and Dad not love me. They always have, even when Johnny was alive, and now I have to wonder if any of that was true, if they really loved me or some image of me—Perfect Jocelyn, The Child That Always Does Just What We Want Her To.

Abby, I'm twenty-three years old, and for twenty-three years I've smiled when I thought they wanted me to smile and worked when I thought they wanted me to work and spoken when I thought they wanted me to speak, and for twenty-three years I've ignored the voice inside me that says do what you want Jocelyn, it's your life, not theirs, but now that voice won't be silenced. It's been growing louder and more insistent, and last night instead of sleeping I thought about Jess in a jail cell and you lying on the family room floor and I knew if I didn't leave I'd die too.

I don't know where I'm going. You cannot imagine how liberating that is to me, to know I can get in my car and drive someplace and not know where I'm going. I'll be in touch when I get to somewhere worth writing from.

I'm sorry to do this to you, just leave without saying good-bye, but I was afraid if I spoke to you, you'd convince me not to go, and I have to, and the sooner the better. I've left a note for Mom and Dad in their room. I figured you'd come to my room to check things out, and that's why I've left this letter for you here.

I do love you, Abby, and I think you have a good chance of making it, if you just hold on. Insist on therapy; don't let Mom and Dad weasel out. Stay healthy, and remember always that you have strength you've never used, and courage, and a real gift for life.

Love,
Jocelyn

Abby: Tell me about the knives, Tim. Tell me what they'll feel like next to my skin.

Tim: You don't need knives. People with strength and courage and a real gift for life don't need knives.

Abby: What if Jocelyn was wrong? What if you're wrong? They're going to be home soon, and they'll find out that Jocelyn's gone, and then what happens? Then what becomes of me?

Tim: Let me tell you something Abby, something it's about time you learned. I don't know what the future holds. Nobody does, not even Johnny, checking in from heaven. Did you think two months ago that Jess would end up in jail, that Jocelyn would turn her back on medical school? Did you honestly think two months ago that you'd be alive today?

Abby: Hold on. I might have guessed about Jess.

Tim: One out of three, Abby. One out of three. Now think of three possibilities for the next two months.

Abby: Right now?

Tim: You have anything better to do?

Abby: Okay. Two months from now I could be dead.

Knives and all. I'd really like to picture myself as a mad slasher, but it just doesn't work.

Tim: All right. Possibility number one is death. What are the other two?

Abby: Things could stay the same. I could stay in my room while Dad keeps on performing surgery and Mom stays in her office or strays out of it.

Tim: In other words, dead or dead.

Abby: Why do you think death is such a comfortable idea for me?

Tim: Possibility number three, Abby.

Abby: Can there be another possibility? I'm not Jess. I'm not Jocelyn.

Tim: There's got to be another possibility. There's got to be an opposite to dead.

Abby: What? Alive?

Tim: It is a possibility.

Abby: You mean I leave my bedroom, start talking to people, to people like the real Tim, show my parents that I'm a human being with feelings and fears and dreams all my own, talk back to a teacher sometime, or try out for the class play, sing, dance, roller-skate my way to happiness?

Tim: Indoor roller-skating. It's hard to roller-skate on ice.

Abby: You're crazy.

Tim: I'm crazy? You try to kill yourself and don't even say a word when your mother drops you off at home and goes on to the office and you say I'm crazy?

Abby: I was scared if she stayed at home with me she'd make me talk to her, make me tell her why I'd tried. I was glad to be alone. Alone is the only way I know how to live.

Tim: There's got to be another way. Other people aren't alone all the time.

101

Abby: Just out of curiosity, what do I do first? Assuming I decide to go for possibility number three.

Tim: Leave your bedroom. Call your parents to tell them Jocelyn's left. Pick up the phone, Abby, and start shaking things up.

Abby: I'm scared.

Tim: That's part of the human condition, Abby. Part of the spirit condition too.

The Most Important Event in My Life
by Abigail Talbott

"Mom, this is Abby."

"Abby, I'm busy now. Can this wait?"

"No Mom, it can't. I have to tell you Jocelyn's left."

"Left? What do you mean by left?"

"She packed her bags and got in her car and drove away. She's gone, Mom."

"When? When did she leave?"

"An hour ago. Maybe more."

"An hour ago, and you're only telling me now? Did she tell you where she's going?"

"She left a note. She says she doesn't know."

"Oh my God."

"Mom, she's twenty-three years old. She knows how to drive."

"I don't need humor right now, Abby. Does your father know yet?"

"No. I called you first."

"This will kill him. He was sure he could convince her to go back to medical school."

"Mom."

"What?"

"What about me, Mom?"

"What do you mean, what about you?"

"You said you were trying to find a therapist for me. Have you, Mom?"

"Abby, I'm sure you understand that these have not been the easiest few days for us. Your father and I have been very worried about Jocelyn."

"I think you should worry about me too, Mom."

"What is that, some kind of a threat? I have to tell you, I'm in no mood for threats."

"It's not a threat, Mom. It's a . . . it's a request."

"I don't know where this sudden infatuation with therapy comes from, but if it's that important to you, go through the phone book and call and make an appointment. I'm sure you'll have just as good luck finding someone for you as your father and I would have."

"Are you telling me to find a therapist for myself?"

"I'm telling you that you chose to call at a lousy time and now I have to call your father and tell him Jocelyn's left home and much as I'd like to make small talk with you, this is neither the time nor the place."

"This is big talk, Mom."

"You know where the phone book is, Abby."

Abby: Now what?

Tim: I don't know. T for Therapists? P for Psychologists?

Abby: You mean I just do it?

Tim: Three possibilities, Abby. Dead, dead, and the phone book.

Abby: But what would I say?

Tim: Say you tried to kill yourself a couple of weeks ago and it occurred to you maybe you should get some help.

Abby: Just like that?

Tim: I can't make the call for you, Abby. Spirits have their limitations.

Abby: Anyone but Doctor Howard, right?

Tim: If you can't trust Jess, who can you trust?

The Most Important Event in My Life—Part Two
by Abigail Talbott

"Hello, Dr. Leibowitz?"

"Yes?"

"My name is Abby Talbott. Abigail Talbott, and, well, I think I need some help."

"What sort of help?"

"Well, a couple of weeks ago, I tried to kill myself, and lately I've been starting to think I really don't want to be dead."

"Are you all right now? Have you just tried suicide?"

"You mean like right now?"

"Yes."

"No, I'm fine. I've been thinking a lot about knives lately, but I don't think I'm going to do anything."

"I think you're right, Abby, and an appointment would be a good idea. What does your schedule look like?"

"I'm free now. I mean for the next few days."

104

"How about four o'clock this afternoon?"

"What? Okay. Sure."

"Do you know how to get to my office?"

"I don't have a car. I'll take a cab."

"Four o'clock then."

"Yes, thank you."

"And Abby, if you start thinking about killing yourself between now and then, seriously thinking about it, call me. Don't hesitate. I'll take your call."

"Thank you. That's very nice of you."

"I'll see you at four, Abby."

"Right. Four. Thank you."

Abby: I did it!

Tim: Three possibilities, Abby. Dead, dead, and alive.

Transcript: Session with Abby Talbott

Dr. Leibowitz: Abby? Come on in.

Abby: Thank you.

Dr. Leibowitz: I wasn't certain how old you'd be, but you're a little younger than I'd anticipated.

Abby: I'm sixteen. Is that too young?

Dr. Leibowitz: No, of course not. But usually with teenagers, I speak to their parents first.

Abby: My parents have been kind of busy lately. They're always busy, they're very busy people, but lately they've been even busier than usual.

Dr. Leibowitz: Because of the holidays?

Abby: Yeah. In a way. I have money to pay for this session, cash I mean, and my parents will pay you if you agree to

105

see me. They want me to be in therapy, they told me so, but it's been hard for them to find someone, so my mother kind of suggested I find someone for myself.

Dr. Leibowitz: *That's interesting. When did she suggest that?*

Abby: *About ten minutes before I called you.*

Dr. Leibowitz: *So you thought it was a good idea too.*

Abby: *I figured why wait.*

Dr. Leibowitz: *How did you happen to pick me?*

Abby: *It was guesswork. I went through the phone book, looking for unfamiliar names, and I didn't know yours, so I figured I'd give you a try. And I guess I liked the fact that you're a woman. Deborah Leibowitz. It sounded right.*

Dr. Leibowitz: *Why was it important that you not know the therapist? Have you been in therapy before?*

Abby: *Not me. My sister Jess. She made the rounds a few years back, and my parents said they wanted me to have a therapist that didn't know Jess. You never saw her, did you?*

Dr. Leibowitz: *No. I checked my records before you came, and I've never seen anyone named Talbott.*

Abby: *Good. My parents will be glad to hear that.*

Dr. Leibowitz: *Why?*

Abby: *It's just Jess didn't turn out too well. She's in jail now. I think my parents figure someone new might do better.*

Dr. Leibowitz: *They told you that?*

Abby: *Not exactly. I heard them talking to my sister Jocelyn about it.*

Dr. Leibowitz: *You have two sisters then, Jess and Jocelyn.*

Abby: *Jocelyn and Jess.*

Dr. Leibowitz: *Is there anyone else in your family? Besides your parents, I mean.*

Abby: *Not exactly. There was a son, Johnny, but he died two years before I was born.*

106

Dr. Leibowitz: *And what do your parents do?*

Abby: *My father's a surgeon and my mother's a lawyer. So they can afford to pay you, if that's what you were worried about.*

Dr. Leibowitz: *What I'm concerned about is your suicide attempt. Could you tell me about it?*

Abby: *What do you want to know?*

Dr. Leibowitz: *Exactly what did you do?*

Abby: *My mother has a lot of prescription sedatives so I took a whole lot of them and washed them down with vodka.*

Dr. Leibowitz: *And someone found you.*

Abby: *My mother. She called for an ambulance and they pumped my stomach at the hospital. I spent the night there, but that was just to be cautious.*

Dr. Leibowitz: *Were you expecting your mother to find you?*

Abby: *Well I knew someone would come home that night, but I didn't know if it would be in time or not. I figured I had a fifty-fifty chance.*

Dr. Leibowitz: *A lot of times when people try to kill themselves with pills they call someone after they take the pills. Did you do that?*

Abby: *No.*

Dr. Leibowitz: *And the suicidal thoughts you were having today. What were they like?*

Abby: *It's hard to explain. Things just haven't been real great with my family lately, and I've been upset. When I tried a couple of weeks ago, it just felt like the right thing to do, but since then I haven't really wanted to die, only sometimes I think about knives, you know, slitting my wrists. I didn't think I'd actually do it, but I worried that I was even thinking about it. I don't want to keep trying and failing. My father thinks I do enough of that as it is.*

Dr. Leibowitz: *Do you want to tell me about your father?*

Abby: *There isn't that much to tell. He's very successful and he expects a lot from people. More from Jocelyn than any-*

107

body else. Actually, the only thing he expects from Jess these days is trouble.

Dr. Leibowitz: *And what does he expect from you?*

Abby: *Not very much.*

Dr. Leibowitz: *Does your mother have high expectations too?*

Abby: *Of Jocelyn? Sure. And I think she'd like not to give up on Jess.*

Dr. Leibowitz: *And what does she expect of you?*

Abby: *I'm not sure. My mother is very busy, so we don't have that much time to talk.*

Dr. Leibowitz: *What did your parents say about your suicide attempt?*

Abby: *Is this what therapy is going to be like? You're just going to keep asking me questions?*

Dr. Leibowitz: *Not exactly. Therapy is a way of helping you find the path you want to take with your life. Right now I'm asking a lot of questions because I want to find out as much as I can about you very fast. Later on, when we know each other better, it'll be more of a dialogue.*

Abby: *It's just I'm not very good at talking.*

Dr. Leibowitz: *I haven't found that at all.*

Abby: *No?*

Dr. Leibowitz: *You seem articulate and self-aware to me. Do you talk much with your friends?*

Abby: *No.*

Dr. Leibowitz: *Do you have a lot of friends?*

Abby: *Not a lot, no.*

Dr. Leibowitz: *Tell me about your best friend.*

Abby: *I guess that's Rachel. We met a long time ago, when we were eleven, and our families were staying at the same hotel one summer. We were all on vacation. Her father was a lot like mine, they're both doctors and everything, and we became instant best friends. Only she lives really far away, so we never see each other. I write to her a lot though, tell her everything that's going on in my life.*

108

Dr. Leibowitz: *Do you have any close friends at school?*

Abby: *I guess I'm shy.*

Dr. Leibowitz: *Do you feel shy?*

Abby: *I don't know. It's more like I don't have anything to say to people. Do you like talking to people?*

Dr. Leibowitz: *Yes, I do, as a matter of fact.*

Abby: *That's good. Then when we're finding my path, you can do a lot of the talking.*

Dr. Leibowitz: *Right now, I think the people I should be talking to are your parents. I'll need to make arrangements with them if we're going to see each other regularly.*

Abby: *This probably isn't the best day for you to call.*

Dr. Leibowitz: *Why not?*

Abby: *My sister Jocelyn left today. That's what I called my mother to tell her when she said I should find a therapist, and she said she'd tell my father, but they're both going to be upset.*

Dr. Leibowitz: *Where did Jocelyn go to?*

Abby: *We don't know.*

Dr. Leibowitz: *She ran away?*

Abby: *Is it running away if you have your own car?*

Dr. Leibowitz: *What exactly did she do?*

Abby: *It wasn't her fault. She was just unhappy in medical school, so she decided to drop out, and she told Mom and Dad, and they got really upset, and they've all been kind of mad at each other, and today Jocelyn decided to leave only she hadn't decided where she was going to go. She left me a note telling me. She left a note for my parents too, only I found mine first, so I called Mom to tell her. I think Dad still thought he could convince her to go back to med school, so he's really going to be upset.*

Dr. Leibowitz: *By upset, do you mean angry?*

Abby: *I guess.*

Dr. Leibowitz: *And you think they're going to be too angry today to talk to me about you?*

109

Abby: I just think tomorrow might be better.

Dr. Leibowitz: Do you think they might take their anger out on you? Are you scared to go home?

Abby: Oh no. They won't be home when I get there, and I'll just stay in my room. My parents don't usually get angry at me.

Dr. Leibowitz: Were they angry at you when you attempted suicide?

Abby: I don't think so.

Dr. Leibowitz: How do you think they felt?

Abby: I don't know. We didn't really talk about it.

Dr. Leibowitz: They must have said something.

Abby: I just think you should talk to them tomorrow.

Dr. Leibowitz: When would be a good time for me to call them?

Abby: You mean together?

Dr. Leibowitz: Yes. Is that a problem?

Abby: It's just my father usually gets up really early to get to the hospital, and lots of times my mother's still asleep when he leaves, or just getting up herself, and you can never be sure exactly when they're going to get home, because they both have a lot of emergencies they have to deal with at work, so they get home really late lots of nights.

Dr. Leibowitz: Would it be better if they called me?

Abby: No.

Dr. Leibowitz: What do you recommend?

Abby: Why don't I give you my mother's work number, and you can call her there tomorrow.

Dec. 28
Dear Rachel,

Well, what was I supposed to say? That if she left it up to them, they'd never get around to calling?

110

We left it that she'd call Mom tomorrow morning, but I should tell them tonight that I went there on my own. I know I should, but it just terrifies me. Mom told me to, but that doesn't mean Dad's going to think it was such a great idea. And today isn't exactly the day I want to take chances with them.

I felt bad telling Dr. Leibowitz about you, but I had to tell her something. Things weren't coming out at all the way I wanted them to, and she kept asking me questions. And what else could I say—the person I talk most with is a boy in my history class only he doesn't know I'm alive so I have these conversations with him on paper when he's now saying he's a spirit who had Christmas with Tiny Tim? I figure my best chance at getting healthy is if Dr. Leibowitz doesn't decide I'm crazy right off the bat.

Maybe Mom and Dad won't come home tonight. There's no reason for them to, with Jocelyn gone. Then it won't be my fault if I didn't tell them about Dr. Leibowitz.

The funny thing is, even though I'm terrified about telling them what I did, I feel a lot better just having talked to Dr. Leibowitz.

I don't want to kill myself. Right now I think I might like being dead, but I don't want to do it.

Maybe Jess will escape from jail, come home, mistake me for Dad, and put me out of my misery.

Abby

Abby: It's 10:15, and neither one of them is back yet.
Tim: What do you expect me to do about it?
Abby: I'm looking for some advice here. Do I call Mom at the office?
Tim: Do you honestly think she's still there?
Abby: Yeah. I don't know.

111

Tim: Do you want to find out that she isn't?

Abby: It's not a big deal. I mean she could be at a party or something.

Tim: And what about your father? Do you think he's at a party or something?

Abby: He's probably sleeping at the hospital. He does that a lot when he's had a heavy day. I can't call him. I'd wake him, if he isn't in surgery right now.

Tim: Not that many people have operations at 10:15 at night.

Abby: They do if there's an emergency. There could have been a car crash, and Dad could be operating on them.

Tim: So what you're saying is neither one of them is going to come home right away, and you can't call either of them, and it's okay for Dr. Leibowitz to call your mother tomorrow and spring it on her that you started therapy on your own.

Abby: Mom told me to. I don't think she'll be too mad.

Tim: So what are you so scared about?

Abby: Did you notice how Dr. Leibowitz kept asking me what they thought about my suicide attempt?

Tim: I'm a spirit, Abby. I don't go with you everywhere you go.

Abby: Well she did.

Tim: Why didn't you tell her the truth?

Abby: What? That I don't know what they thought, because they haven't gotten around to discussing it with me? That I'm so unimportant to them that it isn't even worth a few minutes of their time to ask me why I wanted to die? That I'm such a nothing, I'm not even an embarrassment to them?

Tim: Calm down. You know they love you.

Abby: I do?

Tim: They gave you the dollhouse.

Abby: Yeah. And they clothed me and sheltered me and signed my report cards.

112

Tim: That's more than they've done for Jess in quite a while.

Abby: I want different parents. I want the kind of parents who are home at 10:15.

Tim: Fine. So go to Woolworth's and buy yourself a set.

Dec. 29
Dear Rachel,

Mom got in last night around 1:00. I was asleep, but I heard her coming in. I never did hear Dad, so I guess he spent the night at the hospital.

I figured Mom would be in an awful mood in the morning, so I got out of bed and met her in the living room. She looked real tired, but I didn't have a lot of options.

I told her Jocelyn's note to her was in her room, and I asked if she'd heard from her. Mom said no. Then Mom asked if Dad was home yet, and I said no, and I hadn't heard from him either. She said fine. I guess she was in no mood to see him either.

Then I said I'd followed her advice and called a therapist on my own and Mom said what, and you could see she was mad. She said it was very late, and she would continue this conversation with me tomorrow evening.

I said that would be okay except the therapist would be calling Mom at the office tomorrow, and I wanted her to know so the call wouldn't surprise her. And Mom said call me about what, so I explained I'd already gone to see her, Dr. Leibowitz, and they had to talk about how many sessions (Dr. Leibowitz told me at least two a week for starters) and cost and whether Mom and Dad approved. And Mom said, "How am I supposed to know if your father approves, we haven't had a chance to talk about it since Jocelyn came home."

I got mad, and I said, "Guess," and Mom stared at me, and I asked her what she had felt when she saw me in the

113

family room that night. Mom said she was too tired to talk to me about it just then, and where did I say Jocelyn had left the note, and I said in her bedroom and went back to my room.

Sometimes I envy Jess. They were never too tired to scream at her.

Abby

Transcript: Session with Abby Talbott

Abby: *It was nice of you to see me again so soon.*

Dr. Leibowitz: *We'll set up a more normal schedule next week. But I thought it would be good if we saw each other before New Year's weekend.*

Abby: *What did my mother say to you?*

Dr. Leibowitz: *What did she tell you?*

Abby: *Not much. Just that she talked to you, and you seemed professional enough, and if I liked you, then I might as well see you. I just thought she might have said something more to you.*

Dr. Leibowitz: *We talked a little bit about you, and about your family.*

Abby: *Did you like her?*

Dr. Leibowitz: *She seemed pleasant enough. She was clearly concerned about you.*

Abby: *Oh?*

Dr. Leibowitz: *You sound surprised.*

Abby: *No, of course not. It's just she's been so busy lately.*

Dr. Leibowitz: *You said that the other day as well, how busy your parents both are. Do you wish sometimes they were less busy, that they had more time to spend with you?*

Abby: *No.*

Dr. Leibowitz: *Why not?*

Abby: *How does this work? The stuff I tell you, do you talk to my parents about it?*

Dr. Leibowitz: *Never. Well, almost never.*

Abby: *Why almost never?*

Dr. Leibowitz: *If you should tell me that you're planning on murdering your parents, and I believed you, then I'd have to tell them what you said. For that matter, if I honestly believed you were about to commit an act of violence against someone, I'd be obliged to inform them. And if I thought you were suicidal, really planning on it, I'd want to speak to your parents. I'd tell you first, but I would suggest your parents be called in so we could all talk about what was going on. Other than that, everything you say to me is confidential.*

Abby: *I wouldn't kill my parents.*

Dr. Leibowitz: *I didn't really think you would.*

Abby: *I don't even think Jess would and she has a lot more reason to be mad at them than I do.*

Dr. Leibowitz: *I'd like to talk to you about Jess. But first, why don't you wish your parents would spend more time with you?*

Abby: *It's not like I'm a kid anymore.*

Dr. Leibowitz: *When you were a kid, did your parents spend a lot of time with you?*

Abby: *I don't know.*

Dr. Leibowitz: *Did you do a lot of things with them? Family trips, things like that?*

Abby: *We did a lot of stuff together before Jocelyn went to college.*

Dr. Leibowitz: *How old were you when Jocelyn left?*

Abby: *I was eleven.*

Dr. Leibowitz: *And it was after that that your parents got so busy?*

Abby: *I guess.*

115

Dr. Leibowitz: *Did it upset you that your parents became so busy?*

Abby: *I don't think so.*

Dr. Leibowitz: *Did you miss Jocelyn? Were the two of you close?*

Abby: *I missed her. Jocelyn was always real good about spending time with me. And she helped me a lot.*

Dr. Leibowitz: *She sounds very nice. How did she help you?*

Abby: *I don't know.*

Dr. Leibowitz: *Did she help you with your schoolwork? She must be bright if she got into medical school.*

Abby: *Yeah, she did. She's a lot older than me, so she knew everything before I had a chance to learn it.*

Dr. Leibowitz: *And did you talk to her about your problems?*

Abby: *Sometimes. I remember once I fell off my bike and hurt myself, and Jocelyn was home, and she cleaned it and bandaged it for me.*

Dr. Leibowitz: *Your parents weren't home?*

Abby: *They were both at work.*

Dr. Leibowitz: *And was there a grown-up in the house to look after you?*

Abby: *We used to have housekeepers, but we could never hold on to any, I think because of Jess, so once I got older Mom just hired people to clean the house a couple of times a week. It was hard, because Mom and Dad liked the fact that Jocelyn had a lot of after-school activities, she was always real busy, but they didn't trust Jess to look after me by herself, only it was hard to get someone to stay with us, since Jess was so hard, so after a while they just figured I could take care of myself and I did. It isn't hard to take care of yourself. Kids do it all the time.*

Dr. Leibowitz: *What was so hard about Jess?*

Abby: *She used to get drunk and she did drugs and she did stuff.*

Dr. Leibowitz: *What kind of stuff?*

116

Abby: *Just bad things.*

Dr. Leibowitz: *Did it scare you, being alone with Jess?*

Abby: *Sometimes.*

Dr. Leibowitz: *Did you tell your parents that?*

Abby: *I thought you said this was going to be a dialogue. You want me to do all the talking again.*

Dr. Leibowitz: *I'm still trying to get to know you.*

Abby: *What difference does it make how I felt about being alone with Jess five years ago? She's in jail now.*

Dr. Leibowitz: *People have histories, Abby. When they first come here, I need to find out as much as I can about those histories, so I can get a good fix on what each person is like, what she's going to want and need from therapy. Since you're still a teenager, your history is mostly that of your childhood. That's why I've been asking questions about you and Jess and Jocelyn.*

Abby: *And my parents.*

Dr. Leibowitz: *And your parents.*

Abby: *Do you have any sisters?*

Dr. Leibowitz: *One brother, younger than me.*

Abby: *What does he do?*

Dr. Leibowitz: *He works with my father. We have a family business.*

Abby: *Kind of like Jocelyn and Dad. My grandfather was a doctor too, and so was my great-grandfather.*

Dr. Leibowitz: *Have you ever thought about being a doctor?*

Abby: *When I was younger, I did for a little bit. But you have to be so smart to get into medical school, you know, like Jocelyn.*

Dr. Leibowitz: *What are your grades like?*

Abby: *They're all in the nineties.*

Dr. Leibowitz: *Really? With grades like that, you should be able to get into a very good premed program.*

Abby: *Really?*

Dr. Leibowitz: *Doesn't your father think so?*

117

Abby: *I don't know. We never really talked about it. Besides, I don't want to be a doctor anymore. If Jocelyn hated medical school, then I'm sure I would. That's one reason why . . .*

Dr. Leibowitz: *One reason why . . .*

Abby: *Why it was so upsetting that Jocelyn dropped out. Because now maybe Dad would decide I should be a doctor, and he'd make me work really hard.*

Dr. Leibowitz: *He doesn't make you work hard now?*

Abby: *No. He doesn't much care. He gets upset if my grades aren't good, he got real mad at me last year when I got an eighty-nine in geometry on my report card, but he doesn't check to make sure I'm doing my homework or anything.*

Dr. Leibowitz: *Did he check on Jocelyn that way?*

Abby: *No, he never had to. Jocelyn always did things out in the open. And everybody loves her. She always got great grades, and she was student-council president, and played first violin in the school orchestra. She went to Yale.*

Dr. Leibowitz: *Do you know where you want to go to college?*

Abby: *I don't know. My father would like me to go to an Ivy League school too, but I don't think he thinks I can get into one.*

Dr. Leibowitz: *Your grades sound good enough.*

Abby: *I don't have any extracurricular activities.*

Dr. Leibowitz: *You don't play the violin?*

Abby: *I've never been very good at playing anything.*

Dr. Leibowitz: *What do you like to do?*

Abby: *I don't know. I write a lot.*

Dr. Leibowitz: *Really? What kinds of things do you write?*

Abby: *Letters. And I write essays. My father told me to, to write essays on the most important event in my life, so if they asked for one with my college application I'd know how to do it, and I've written a lot of them.*

Dr. Leibowitz: *What was the most important event in your life?*

Abby: *I haven't decided yet. Every time I finish one, I think* *of another event. Of course most of them I could never send to a college.*

Dr. Leibowitz: *Why not?*

Abby: *They're too personal. And what I think of as an important event, they might not think is.*

Dr. Leibowitz: *Tell me about one of your essays. What was the most important event?*

Abby: *I wrote once about a picnic we all went on together. You know. That kind of thing.*

Dr. Leibowitz: *Was it a nice picnic? Did you all have a good time?*

Abby: *It was a very nice picnic.*

Dec. 30
Dear Rachel,

So what was I supposed to tell her about? Johnny's little visit? The time I got drunk? Or when Dad threw the TV set? Or maybe she would have liked to hear about when Jess told me to pee on Johnny's grave.

Now that I think about it, she probably would have liked that.

The funny thing was she seemed more interested in me than she was in Jocelyn or even Jess. I would have thought a therapist would have just loved to hear about Jess.

Nobody's ever been really interested in me before. I know, she's getting paid to be interested, but I really think if she wasn't, she'd just decide not to see me. Who wants to be bored twice a week just for some money?

She said she'd like to see my New Year's resolutions, if I make any. I never have before, but this year seems like a good time to try. It's like insurance against killing myself. No point making resolutions if you're going the slit-wrist way in a week.

Abby

119

New Year's Resolutions

I resolve to get better grades.

I resolve to actually talk to Tim. The real one.

New Year's Resolutions

I resolve to get better grades.

I resolve to start a conversation with Tim.

I resolve to eat more vegetables.

New Year's Resolutions

I resolve to get better grades.

I resolve to be more outgoing at school.

I resolve to take tennis lessons.

I resolve to write a really good essay about the most important event in my life so I'll have one all ready for my college applications. Maybe even this weekend.

I resolve to take more walks when the weather is nicer.

120

New Year's Resolutions

I resolve to get grades so good that even Dad will think so.

I resolve to get Tim to talk to me, really talk, so I can think of him as a real person and stop writing dialogue for him where he tells me about knives.

I resolve to be more like Jocelyn used to be, popular and busy and successful.

I resolve to make a friend, a real one, someone who calls me sometimes and we talk about boys and what's going on at school.

I resolve to hate myself less.

The Most Important Event in My Life
by Abigail Talbott

When I was eight years old, my mother asked me if I would like to join the local Brownie troop.

Oh, how excited I was to be asked. Both my sisters, Jocelyn and Jessica, had been Brownies and then Girl Scouts when they were younger, and, of course, as their kid sister, I idolized them. But I had never dreamed that one day I would be old enough to follow in their footsteps.

What made the idea even sweeter was that my mother herself had been first a Brownie and then a Girl Scout. She regaled me with stories about her days in scouting when we went shopping for my Brownie uniform. I was one happy little girl that day, eager to join in a tradition that extended so far back in my family.

No, this won't do. I'm not ready yet to write for other people's eyes.

12/31
Abby—

I know you took a solemn vow on Johnny's grave never to write to me, but it's been almost two weeks since I've heard anything from Jocelyn, and that might not seem like a long time to you, but you've never been in jail.

I know something is wrong, and I wish you'd break that solemn vow and let me know what's happening. It doesn't help that her last communication with me had to do with your suicide attempt, and I haven't heard anything from anybody since (not even a card at Christmas—God I hate Mom and Dad) and Jocelyn said you'd be all right, and there was little risk of brain damage, but still little risk isn't no risk, and is that what's happening (and if it is, why the hell am I writing to you, my sister the vegetable)?

Jocelyn are you there? Are you reading Abby's mail to her? If you are, will you please write to me?

Look, whoever is actually reading this letter, I know I haven't done anything right in my life since Johnny was born, and maybe before then and I just don't remember (there's a lot I don't remember after then either, thanks to the blessed properties of drugs and drink), and I've been cut out of the collective consciousness of the Talbott family, but I do exist and I am a member and it is terrifying to be stuck in this cell waiting only for the day when I go to court, admit guilt, and get sentenced to a year or two in a state prison, knowing that something is going on with the only people I ever loved (so what if they never loved me, when you're desperate, you're desperate), and instead of being cut off almost completely, you've been cut off completely, and you don't know if it's something new you've done or whether they've just gotten so busy with their own lives, they've forgotten you exist (God knows, they've wished for years that I didn't), and Jocelyn for all her holier-than-thou attitude at least used to apply some Christian charity to me and tell me how everybody was and now she's vanished too and I'm starting to panic, anybody out there listening? panic thinking something horrible must have happened, and what is it, is Dad all right, the way he lives, he'll be dead of a heart attack before he's sixty, or is it Mom, run off finally, or Jocelyn, although I can't picture anything really bad happening to Jocelyn, let alone Jocelyn doing something really bad, or worse still, has something happened to Abby and nobody's telling me as a kind of punishment, well she wouldn't care so why bother telling her, let her rot in jail, serves her right, never any good, maybe after a couple of years in prison she'll forget us altogether and not bother us anymore. I'm sorry I bothered you, I'm sorry I asked for money all the time, I'm sorry I've thrown my life away, but God, please don't forget me, don't let me just lie here not knowing, I'm not that bad a person, not really, and I want to be better, I want to be more like Jocelyn, don't laugh, I can want that, just write and tell me everybody is all right or everybody isn't all

123

right, but at least tell me, I need to know, I am a Talbott, I am a member of this family, and I need to know, God is there anyone out there, just write or call or do something, because the more scared I get the harder it gets and things are hard enough, I don't need harder please.

Jess

Transcript: Session with Abby Talbott

Abby: *Can I talk to you about Jess?*

Dr. Leibowitz: *You can talk to me about anything.*

Abby: *Really? Anything?*

Dr. Leibowitz: *Anything.*

Abby: *That's interesting. That I could do that, I mean, just talk to you about anything. I probably knew that, but it still feels strange to actually say it.*

Dr. Leibowitz: *The idea behind therapy is it's a safe place, a place where you can talk about anything, see how things sound, find out things about yourself.*

Abby: *I think I know enough about myself already. It's Jess I need to talk about.*

Dr. Leibowitz: *What about her?*

Abby: *I got a letter from her a couple of days ago, and I never thought I'd say this about her, but it was sad.*

Dr. Leibowitz: *In what way?*

Abby: *Well she's in jail and she's going to plea-bargain and go to prison soon and Jocelyn used to write to her, and she was the only one who did, but now Jocelyn's gone into deep hiding someplace, I haven't heard from her either, and Jess is really scared.*

Dr. Leibowitz: *Do your parents maintain contact with Jess?*

Abby: *No. They cut her off completely a couple of years ago.*

124

Jess keeps after them anyway, mostly for money, and she writes to me, only I don't answer her letters. I never felt I had to, since Jocelyn did, but now Jocelyn isn't, and Jess is my sister, and I don't know what to do.

Dr. Leibowitz: *What do you want to do?*

Abby: *Why?*

Dr. Leibowitz: *Because that's a factor. Your wishes count.*

Abby: *Oh yeah. I don't know. I've never wanted to do much of anything where Jess was concerned except maybe hide my head in the sand.*

Dr. Leibowitz: *What does Jess want from you?*

Abby: *A letter. She says she's worried because she hasn't heard from Jocelyn since I took all those pills and she's worried if I'm okay. She even said she was worried about Mom and Dad and Jocelyn, and I don't know.*

Dr. Leibowitz: *Is there a reason why you don't write to Jess?*

Abby: *What do you mean?*

Dr. Leibowitz: *Did you promise your parents that you wouldn't?*

Abby: *No. Jess has always been bad, and even when Jocelyn was living at home, Jess was drinking and doing drugs, but once Jocelyn left, things got worse. Jess ran away for the first time, and then she came back and left and came back and left a few times and then Mom and Dad told her she could never come back, they no longer wanted to have anything to do with her.*

Dr. Leibowitz: *Even if she straightened herself out?*

Abby: *I don't know. The odds were kind of against that. Anyway, Mom told me that if Jess ever called collect I shouldn't accept the charge, and if she ever just called I should just hang up on her, and of course she did both, and I did what Mom said. Then Jess started writing to me, because she knew I got home first, and Mom and Dad wouldn't know, only I never answered any of her letters.*

125

*Jocelyn did though, so I knew what was going on with Jess,
which was nothing good.*

Dr. Leibowitz: *If your parents haven't forbidden you to
write, then you're choosing not to yourself.*

Abby: *I don't know what to say to her.*

Dr. Leibowitz: *You could reassure her that you're all right.*

Abby: *I could.*

Dr. Leibowitz: *But . . .*

Abby: *But then I'd have to tell her about Jocelyn.*

Dr. Leibowitz: *Why does that disturb you?*

Abby: *I don't know. A lot of reasons.*

Dr. Leibowitz: *Such as . . .*

Abby: *Do you have to do that? Ask me those little prompting
questions—but, such as? I may not have this therapy business all worked out yet, but I do know I'm either going to
tell you something or I'm not going to bring it up, and
maybe I can't get the words out as fast as you'd like, but
that doesn't mean I'm not going to say them, and I don't
need you pushing me along, all right?*

Dr. Leibowitz: *All right.*

Abby: *I'm sorry.*

Dr. Leibowitz: *What about? If that isn't too much of a
prompting question.*

Abby: *I didn't mean to be rude.*

Dr. Leibowitz: *You weren't. You're possibly the least rude
person I've ever met.*

Abby: *It's just I get so mad sometimes.*

Dr. Leibowitz: *At who? (laughs) God, you've made me
nervous. Half my professional style depends on prompting
questions.*

Abby: *I don't want to talk about who I'm mad at. I want
to talk about Jess. Okay, I'm mad at Jess. She used to do
terrible things to me, destroy my toys, hit me. She's five
years older than me, and she used to hurt me. I was always
scared of her. Sometimes she'd be nice, but even then I was
scared because she could just turn on me with no warning,*

126

play with me one minute and hit me the next. Jocelyn used to warn me, say I shouldn't have anything to do with Jess, but I was lonely, and Jess had this way of smiling and pretending she liked me and the next thing I'd know, she'd be on top of me, kicking me.

Dr. Leibowitz: *Did your parents protect you?*

Abby: *Sure, sometimes. Sometimes Jess would be so out of control she'd start beating me when they were around, and then one of them would pull her off of me, and they always knew Jess was to blame, they never thought I provoked her, so they'd punish Jess, but it didn't matter. I remember once when I was about eight, Dad was home alone when it happened, and he . . . well when he got mad at Jess it was pretty scary, and I was sure Jess would kill me the next time we were alone, but she didn't blame me either. I was just a stage prop. Dad didn't ask me if I was all right, and I wasn't, Jess gave me a bloody nose, but it was all just between him and Jess.*

Dr. Leibowitz: *That must have made you very angry.*

Abby: *Sometimes. Mostly it was okay, because I knew that was how it was, that nobody knew I was around. Nobody cares. Sometimes I think they even love Jess more than me because . . . I'm sorry. I know I shouldn't cry.*

Dr. Leibowitz: *You can cry whenever you need to.*

Abby: *Dad doesn't like it if I cry. He says I'm a crybaby when I do.*

Dr. Leibowitz: *Your father isn't here. He won't know that you cried.*

Abby: *(sobs)*

Dr. Leibowitz: *It's all right. You have a lot of tears inside you.*

Abby: *He cries once a year. On the day Johnny died. We go to Johnny's grave and Dad cries so hard it's . . . (sobs)*

Dr. Leibowitz: *Do you feel that your father loves Johnny more than he loves you?*

Abby (laughing and crying): *What? Are you crazy? Of*

127

course I do. Dad loves Johnny even more than he loves Jocelyn, and Jocelyn's the only person on earth he loves.
Dr. Leibowitz: *He doesn't love you at all?*
Abby: *I don't know. I guess if you asked him, he'd say he loves me.*
Dr. Leibowitz: *Would he say he loves Jess?*
Abby: *I don't think so.*
Dr. Leibowitz: *So if he says he loves you, he probably does.*
Abby: *Then why doesn't he act like he does?*
Dr. Leibowitz: *Because he's an imperfect person.*
Abby: *(laughs)*
Dr. Leibowitz: *I gather you knew that already.*

Jan. 3
Dear Jess,

I'm sorry I haven't written to you

Jan. 3
Dear Jess,

No, I'm not brain damaged, or at least no more than you'd expect coming from this family. And something is going on, but not what you think. Jocelyn dropped out of medical school, and you can imagine how Dad felt about that, and Jocelyn packed her bags and left home and she hasn't bothered to tell any of us where she's gone. Very un-Jocelyn.

Dad and Mom are behaving in character though. They don't even mention her. This would be tricky, since they don't mention you either, and they never mentioned me, but they're handling it by never being at home. I think what you said about Mom must be right, and I'm starting to wonder about Dad too.

I'm in therapy. I found myself a therapist, since Mom

128

and Dad were too distracted by Jocelyn to do anything about it, a woman named Dr. Leibowitz, who seems to think we're all crazy (I wonder where she got that idea). I'm seeing her twice a week, and I talk to her about everything. She sends the bills to Mom, who I guess is paying promptly enough.

Just because I've written you this letter, don't expect me to turn into Jocelyn and write you regularly. I'm not Jocelyn and I'm never going to be, and you scare me Jess, and I don't think you ever scared Jocelyn. So I'll write you when it's important for you to know something (like I'm not brain dead), and when I hear from Jocelyn I'll let you know, but that's it.

Abby

1/6
Abby—

Thanks for the letter. It meant a lot to me.

What do you mean what I said about Mom?

My court date is set for Feb. 13. My lawyer thinks they'll include my jail time as part of my sentence, and with good behavior, I could be out in a year.

I'm sorry I scare you. I scare me even more.

Jess

January 15
Dear Abby,

I'm sorry I've taken so long to write and let you know how things are with me. When I got into my car that day, I had no idea where I'd end up, or even if I'd ever end up anyplace.

129

I'd never had Dad angry at me before. Of course I'd seen what he could be like, but he's always been so proud of me. It terrified me, the way he was acting, and I knew the only way I could survive was to get as far away as possible.

For a week, I just drove, not caring where I was going. New Year's Eve I spent at a Howard Johnson's in Dearborn, Michigan. Two days later, I was in Tulsa, Oklahoma, where I spent the night crying and the following day asking myself what it was I wanted out of life.

Who would have thought I'd find my way in Tulsa?

I got back into my car and drove to Boston. I got there at four o'clock in the afternoon, two days later, and I sat in my car, shaking with terror and relief, until Roger came home from work.

I met him outside, and we walked up to his apartment. Five minutes later, we were in bed together, and I knew I'd found my way home.

We got married yesterday, Abby. I only wish you could have been here. It was a nothing ceremony, just a few words in front of strangers, but I knew it was the most important day of my life. For years I've dreamed of what I want my marriage to be like, open, caring, with love and laughter, and I know with Roger I'll have all that and more.

Roger and I have talked a lot about our future. We've agreed we both want children and we want them while we're still young (of course that was one reason why we broke up in the first place—my determination to get through medical school before starting a family), so we've already started trying for a baby. It's my dream to have one by Thanksgiving.

What I'm about to ask of you is unfair, but I'm not ready to tell Mom and Dad any of this yet, so please keep this letter secret. I think I need to feel just a little more married before I let them know, or maybe I have to be pregnant to tell them. They both felt I could do "better" than Roger, and I'm still feeling fragile (although very very happy), and not ready to face their disapproval.

But I want you to be happy for me. Maybe you could visit us over spring vacation. Roger's apartment isn't very big, but once we know for sure I'm pregnant, we'll start looking for a better place (thank God for my trust fund; it's going to make our lives so much easier). But even if we haven't moved, there's a sofa bed in our living room, and we'd both love to see you.

Please write and tell me how everyone is. I think about you all the time, hoping that you're all right. This is terribly premature, but when we have our baby, we'd like you to be its godmother.

Love,
Jocelyn

Jan. 17
Dear Rachel,

Godmother? Is she crazy? I'm still learning how to be a sister, and I haven't even begun on daughter yet, and now I'm supposed to be a godmother?

Sometimes I think Jocelyn is the craziest of all of us. Mom and Dad didn't just think she could do better than Roger. They thought Roger was a total waste, nothing more than a nice guy, an insurance salesman. And now Jocelyn thinks she can have a baby with him, bring it home for Thanksgiving, and then what—Dad gets a new Johnny and all is forgiven?

She didn't mention a thing about Jess either. Jocelyn has no idea how important she is to everybody else.

You know something. I don't envy her baby one bit.

Abby

131

Jan. 18
Dear Jess,

I thought you'd like to know I heard from Jocelyn today and she's in Boston and seems to be okay.

I'm okay too.

I hope your court date goes all right.

Abby

Transcript: Session with Abby Talbott

Abby: *Am I wrong? Or is Jocelyn not doing what she should?*

Dr. Leibowitz: *Do you want an opinion or do you want to vent?*

Abby: *An opinion.*

Dr. Leibowitz: *Jocelyn should tell your parents. It isn't fair to put you in the middle this way.*

Abby: *All my life I've been told how perfect Jocelyn is. Not just by my parents, but at school. I idolized her. Jocelyn was never supposed to do anything wrong, just like Jess wasn't supposed to do anything right.*

Dr. Leibowitz: *And what about you?*

Abby: *I wasn't supposed to do anything. I think my father kind of equates me with Roger.*

Dr. Leibowitz: *Do you think your father will love you more now that Jocelyn has proved she's imperfect by his standards?*

Abby: *(cries)*

Dr. Leibowitz: *Would you like that? For your father to love you more?*

Abby: *(crying) It scares me.*

Dr. Leibowitz: *Why?*

Abby: *(crying) If Dad loves me more, he'll expect me to be like Jocelyn, and I can't be, and I'll disappoint him, and he'll hate me like he hates Jess.*

Dr. Leibowitz: *Even if that's true, why can't you be like Jocelyn?*

132

Abby: *I'm not smart enough.*

Dr. Leibowitz: *You get great grades. You're a very smart girl, Abby.*

Abby: *But Jocelyn's perfect in so many ways. She's popular. Everybody likes her.*

Dr. Leibowitz: *Jocelyn is obviously more outgoing than you are. But that doesn't mean you can't have friends, just the same as Jocelyn.*

Abby: *Jocelyn doesn't have friends.*

Dr. Leibowitz: *What?*

Abby: *Nobody close. She told me that once.*

Dr. Leibowitz: *So you think you can't be as popular as someone without any friends?*

Abby: *Jocelyn has friends. People always like her. But she doesn't have anyone she can confide in. That's why she confides in me, because she doesn't have anyone else who could really understand.*

Dr. Leibowitz: *The way you have Rachel.*

Jan. 19
Dear Rachel,

What should I have said? Sometimes I think Dr. Leibowitz actually respects me. I can't risk losing that. What could I possibly replace it with?

Abby: Notice how we haven't talked much lately?

Tim: I was wondering if you'd forgotten all about me.

Abby: No. I've just been needing you less.

Tim: Fine with me. Us spirits don't stay unemployed very long.

Abby: I need to figure out what to tell Dr. Leibowitz about Rachel.

Tim: What's wrong with the truth?

133

Abby: A lot and you know it.

Tim: Have you told her about me?

Abby: That's different.

Tim: How?

Abby: For starters because I've almost forgotten about you. You're just not that important to me anymore. When I need to talk to someone, I have Dr. Leibowitz. And she doesn't tell me about spending Christmas with Tiny Tim.

Tim: I don't know Dr. Leibowitz, but from all I've heard about her, she's pretty trustworthy. I think you can take the chance.

Abby: But what if she doesn't like me anymore?

Tim: You'll survive. Nobody's liked you up until now and you survived.

Abby: Not real well.

Tim: Take the chance, Abby. Or do you want to spend the rest of your life not taking chances?

Jan. 21
Dear Rachel,

If I tell Dr. Leibowitz about you, I'm so scared I'll lose you. And if I lose you, what will I have left?

Abby

Transcript: Session with Abby Talbott

Dr. Leibowitz: Abby, you've been very quiet today.
Abby: There's something on my mind.
Dr. Leibowitz: Do you want to talk about it?
Abby: No.
Dr. Leibowitz: All right.
Abby: Do you mean that?
Dr. Leibowitz: Sure.

134

Abby: Don't you want to make me talk about it?

Dr. Leibowitz: I want you to feel you can talk about it. But I'm not going to force you to. What good would that do?

Abby: Do you like me?

Dr. Leibowitz: Yes, as a matter of fact. I like you a lot.

Abby: Do you have a lot of friends?

Dr. Leibowitz: I have three friends I'm very close to, and several other friends I enjoy spending time with.

Abby: Did you ever not have friends?

Dr. Leibowitz: When I was twelve, I had a best friend I loved, and then we had a big fight and stopped being friends. That happens a lot when you're twelve, you're growing up and ready to move to different friendships, but of course I didn't know that and I was devastated.

Abby: I've always wished I had friends. I was always jealous of girls who had them.

Dr. Leibowitz: It must be hard for you when your one really close friend lives so far away.

Abby: That's what I need to talk about.

Dr. Leibowitz: I'm listening.

Abby: You know how I told you I confide in Rachel, tell her everything that's going on.

Dr. Leibowitz: Yes.

Abby: That isn't exactly true.

Dr. Leibowitz: Do you mean you don't send her all the letters you write to her? Or you don't tell her everything in the letters you do send?

Abby: When we met that summer we really did become instant best friends. I've never met anybody I liked so much so soon. When I got home, I wrote her a letter, and she wrote back right away, so I wrote her again, and she wrote back only it took a little longer, and then I wrote a third time, and she never wrote back. So I wrote her three more letters, and she never answered any of them.

Dr. Leibowitz: What did you do then?

135

her an expensive present so she'd have to write back, but Mom told me not to. She said some friendships just can't survive long distance, and just because I enjoyed writing letters didn't mean other people did. But I kept on writing the letters because I didn't have anyone else to talk to. Jocelyn started college that year, not that I'd talked that much to her either, and I certainly wasn't going to make Jess my confidante, and I'd never had any friends at school, not really. I wanted to, but I couldn't exactly bring people home. My parents were never in, and Jess . . . well you always had the feeling she was dangerous. She set fire to things, and tore stuff up, and I wasn't about to have everyone in school know what she was like. So all I had was Rachel, but I knew I couldn't keep on writing her if she'd never write back, I was desperate, but not that desperate, so I wrote her letters never intending to mail them. She probably doesn't even remember that I'm alive, and I wouldn't recognize her if we ever ran into each other, but I've been writing her letters that tell her everything that happens in my family and how I feel about it. Until I started therapy, she was the only person I was ever really honest with, and I wasn't really honest with you either, since I told you we were best friends and we're not.

Dr. Leibowitz: *Why did you tell me that?*

Abby: *Because I sounded so damn pathetic otherwise. And now I must sound even more so.*

Dr. Leibowitz: *I don't think of you as pathetic.*

Abby: *You don't?*

Dr. Leibowitz: *Lonely, sure. Boxed in and afraid of getting out. But not pathetic.*

Abby: *You don't think it's sick I write letters never intending to send them to someone who doesn't even remember me?*

Dr. Leibowitz: *For all you know, she does remember you, but that's beside the point. You use the letters as a diary. That's fine. I have a friend who goes on exotic vacations, saves up for them for years so she can go to countries where*

136

you have to get twelve different vaccines, and she can't keep a travel diary, so she writes me letters instead. Every day she adds on to her letter. She's never mailed me one. Sometimes she makes a copy and gives it to me after she gets back, but the letters are her way of keeping a record about the trip in a way she finds comfortable.

Abby: *Is that one of those three close friends of yours?*

Dr. Leibowitz: *She sure is.*

Abby: *It doesn't bother you that she uses you that way?*

Dr. Leibowitz: *It never even occurred to me to be bothered.*

Abby: *How do you make friends?*

Dr. Leibowitz: *You reach out to people, show them you like them, that you share common interests. It doesn't happen overnight. Good friendships take a long time simmering.*

Abby: *I reached out to Rachel.*

Dr. Leibowitz: *It's hard when you're eleven and it's a long-distance friendship. I think you'd do better now with friends. You have more to offer.*

Abby: *I wish I knew what.*

Dr. Leibowitz: *You look like someone who could make a good list. Why don't you go home this evening and make a list of all your best qualities.*

Abby: *(laughs) That'll be a short one.*

Dr. Leibowitz: *I expect to see at least ten things on that list. Bring it the next time you come.*

Abby: *You don't mind that I lied to you?*

Dr. Leibowitz: *I'm human. I love the idea that people walk in here and trust me immediately based on my winning smile. But I'd be a fool to think it happens that way every time, and I'm not a fool. Trust can take time.*

Abby: *Do you trust me less now? You just found out I lied about something.*

Dr. Leibowitz: *Good question. I think I'll listen a little more carefully to you from now on. You have unexpected complexities. I think I like that in you.*

137

My Ten Best Qualities

1. I'm inoffensive.

2. I'm quiet. I don't think that's the same as inoffensive.

3. I'm a good student. I get very good grades no matter what Dad says.

4. I'm loyal. I must be, or else I would have packed my bags and gotten out of here a long time ago.

5. This is kind of fun. I'm modest.

6. I'm neat. I always put my things away and I have nice hand writing.

7. I'm tenacious. I've already written eleven essays about the most important event in my life, and while I couldn't use any of them (except maybe the family picnic one and even that would take a lot of explaining), that must show once I start something I don't give up on it easily. Look at all those last wills and testaments I wrote before I was finally satisfied.

8. I don't drink or take drugs
(except when I'm trying to kill
myself). Also, I'm not a violent
person.

9. I'm running out of good things to
say about myself. I should have
saved the handwriting one and
used it, but it didn't seem like
very much at the time. I bet
lots of perfectly awful people
have had good handwriting.
I'm a good listener. That's a
real virtue, especially if you
want to make friends, because
most people really like talking
about themselves. Look at how
Jocelyn confides in me, even
though I'm seven years younger.
I bet if I had friends, I'd
listen to them all the time,
and that would make them feel
good about themselves, and
then they'd like me too. I
like that one. I just wish I'd
thought to start my list with
it, instead of inoffensive,
which I probably wouldn't
even think of as a

virtue if I weren't related to
Jess.

10. One more. I want it to be a
good one too. I wish I'd
written smart instead of good
student. If I ever make
this list up again, I'll do
a better job of it. I'm funny?
I think I am, but that's
the kind of thing modest
people shouldn't say unless
they have a lot of proof,
which I don't, since I never
talk to anybody for them to
find out that I'm funny.
Damn. I know. I'm self-
sufficient. I've got to be
the most self-sufficient
person in the universe. Look
at me. I've been feeding
myself for years, and I live
in my bedroom, asking for
nothing. Self-sufficient and
smart (well, good grades) and
loyal and a good listener. I
sound a little bit like a cocker
spaniel, but that might not be
bad either. If I were a difficult person, I think I'd like
having a friend like me.

Abby: So why don't you like me?
Tim: You're asking the wrong Tim.

Feb. 4
Dear Jocelyn,

I'm sorry I haven't written you sooner. Your letter took me aback, and then I got busy with schoolwork and therapy. Becoming a sane person is very time-consuming.

Congratulations on marrying Roger. I was always sorry that the two of you split up. I liked the way Roger seemed so sane, which would be a nice change of pace for our family. I don't know what kind of godmother I'll make, but I'm flattered you thought of me for the job.

I wrote to Jess to tell her I'd heard from you, since she was worried when she didn't hear from you for a couple of weeks. She has a court date Feb. 13 and it would mean a lot to her if you wrote to her (or called her) before then. For all I know, you already have, but just in case.

The only person I told about your getting married was my therapist, but I can tell her anything and she won't tell Mom and Dad. I like her a lot. I found her myself the very day you left, when I figured out Mom and Dad weren't going to do it for me. One of the things therapy has taught me is I'm a very self-sufficient person. I talk to her about almost everything and she tells me I'm not crazy. I like hearing that.

Anyway, I think you should tell Mom and Dad you're married (not that you've asked me). If it's something you're proud of, why keep it secret? Dad can't be any angrier at you than he already is. And Mom, I think, will be pleased. Besides, it isn't fair making me keep such a big secret.

Let me know how you are.

Love,
Abby

141

2/14
Abby—

One and a half to three, with jail time counting in my
sentence. My lawyer says with time off for good behavior
I could get paroled in nine months.

I really like my lawyer. He's very busy (public defenders
have a lot of public to defend these days), but he talked to
me seriously a couple of times about my life and what I
could still make of it. He says the state prison has an AA
group and that I'd be a natural for it. He also says I could
study for my high school equivalency exam while I'm in
prison, and if I could just keep myself drug free and reacti-
vate my brain, there's nothing I couldn't do with my life.

He made it sound so easy. I know it would be a lot
harder than that, maybe close to impossible, but for the
first time I don't think it is impossible. And God, I love the
idea of what it would do to Mom and Dad if I made something of my life. Especially with Jocelyn so determined to
have baby after baby (she wrote to me and told me all
about it—Roger's such a jerk I think they'll be very happy
together) and you digesting Mom's pill collection. Not that
I want you to keep doing that. I'd just like to come in
second in the family for a change.

Do me a favor and tell Mom what's happened. Not the
stuff about AA, but my sentence. I'd write to tell her but
when I do, she sends my letters back to me unopened. But
even so, I think she'd like to know.

Jess

Transcript: Session with Abby Talbott

Abby: *What kind of a mother turns her back on her daughter
so completely?*

142

Dr. Leibowitz: *That's such a loaded question I can only assume you don't expect an answer.*

Abby: *When I have kids, I'm going to love them forever, no matter what they're like. I'm a loyal person, you know.*

Dr. Leibowitz: *And you don't think your mother is?*

Abby: *No. I don't know. She's loyal to her job, she's there all the time, and she's loyal to Jocelyn, at least she's mentioning her again, even though Dad's still hysterical that she got married, especially to Roger. And in a way she's loyal to Dad.*

Dr. Leibowitz: *Is she loyal to you?*

Abby: *I don't remember the last time we really talked. I was afraid after I tried to kill myself that Mom would insist on talking to me, and I didn't know what I'd say, because there were so many different reasons why I didn't want to live, and most of them I couldn't begin to tell her, but even then . . . She's never asked me about it. Once, she asked if I liked you, and I said yes, and that ended that. I guess she's loyal to me. She isn't disloyal, if that's the same thing.*

Dr. Leibowitz: *Do you think she loves you?*

Abby: *You expect me to start crying again, don't you?*

Dr. Leibowitz: *You know where the tissues are.*

Abby: *I'm not going to cry. I stopped crying over Mom a long time ago. Like around birth.*

Dr. Leibowitz: *Why?*

Abby: *Why? God, you drive me crazy sometimes.*

Dr. Leibowitz: *My mother can still make me cry. Mothers have that kind of power over daughters.*

Abby: *Mothers you care about do. Mothers who care about you do.*

Dr. Leibowitz: *And you don't care about each other?*

Abby: *No.*

Dr. Leibowitz: *Not at all?*

Abby: *What's your point?*

Dr. Leibowitz: *I like the idea of mothers and daughters* caring about each other. So if you and your mother still have any feeling about each other, then I think it's a good idea if it grows. But if all feeling really is dead, there's no point trying to bring it back to life.

Abby: All right. There's got to be some feeling. She did call for the ambulance after all.

Dr. Leibowitz: That's it?

Abby: I never see her. She's always at the office or out of the office, but she's never at home. Sometimes I think she's scared to be home.

Dr. Leibowitz: Has she told you that?

Abby: She can't tell me anything if she isn't home to tell it.

Transcript: Session with Abby Talbott

Dr. Leibowitz: I've been thinking about you and your mother.

Abby: On your own time?

Dr. Leibowitz: Yeah, I suppose so. At breakfast this morning, and yesterday in the shower. On my own time.

Abby: Do you do that a lot? Think about your clients on your own time?

Dr. Leibowitz: I think about some of them more than others.

Abby: And I'm one of the ones you think about?

Dr. Leibowitz: You're a very special girl, Abby. Naturally I think about you.

Abby: Oh. Really?

Dr. Leibowitz: Really. Now may I tell you what I was thinking?

Abby: Sure.

Dr. Leibowitz: I started with the premise that you and your mother do have feelings for each other, but neither of you knows how to express them.

Abby: So what do you want me to do? Write an essay for Mother's Day?

Dr. Leibowitz: *Is that a question or a comment?*

Abby: *Sorry.*

Dr. Leibowitz: *This is what I decided in the shower yesterday. Part of the problem between you and your mother is you hardly know each other.*

Abby: *That's not my fault.*

Dr. Leibowitz: *No, it isn't. May I speak frankly?*

Abby: *I'd like that.*

Dr. Leibowitz: *I don't know your parents, but I sense strongly that they're closed-off people. Maybe things would have been different if Johnny had lived, or if Jess hadn't been so difficult, but for whatever reasons they've pulled themselves away from positive feelings for the rest of their family. A lot of that is never going to change. But that doesn't mean they don't love you. They don't know how to show it, and I don't think they'll ever be demonstrative, but they do love you.*

Abby: *So where does that leave me?*

Dr. Leibowitz: *An excellent question, and one I thought about a lot this morning. And I decided you had two choices. There may be more that I couldn't come up with, so two will have to do.*

Abby: *Two.*

Dr. Leibowitz: *Any problem with that?*

Abby: *There was a moment when I decided I had three choices, dead, dead, or alive. I don't know whether two is better or worse.*

Dr. Leibowitz: *Hear the choices and then decide.*

Abby: *Okay.*

Dr. Leibowitz: *Choice number one—you can leave everything as is. You stay in your room, your parents stay out of the house, you see each other occasionally, probably for the rest of your life. As you know, it could be worse. Keep your distance, and you'll never be cut off, the way Jess and now apparently Jocelyn have been. It's safe, and I wouldn't try to talk you out of it.*

145

Abby: That's exactly what you're trying to do.

Dr. Leibowitz: I prefer to think I'm offering alternatives that might not have occurred to you.

Abby: Are you like this with your friends?

Dr. Leibowitz: Them I offer unsolicited advice. Why not? If they're going to be friends with a therapist, they'd better come to expect it.

Abby: (laughs)

Dr. Leibowitz: The second alternative is you go to them.

Abby: No.

Dr. Leibowitz: You make the first move. They're not going to. You can hold your breath until you turn purple, you can try to kill yourself on the family room floor, and these people aren't going to make the first move. So if there's going to be any movement, it's got to be up to you.

Abby: That's not fair.

Dr. Leibowitz: No, it isn't.

Abby: Why do I have to be the one? I'm the kid. They're the grown-ups.

Dr. Leibowitz: You have to be the one because it's to your benefit if it happens. Maybe theirs too, but definitely yours.

Abby: Are you sure?

Dr. Leibowitz: Abby, you're a wonderful girl, but you don't know it. You don't know it because your parents have failed to show you how wonderful you are. They've failed to show it because they've cut themselves off from you. Now you might be able to find your way back to yourself without their help. Being in therapy is one way. But if you can just break through that wall your parents have built up, then you can see that they do love you and you are wonderful.

Abby: But what if they don't love me?

Dr. Leibowitz: Any time you open yourself up, you risk getting hurt. And the decision is yours. Stay in your room, keep things the way they are, you won't be hurt any more than you have been. Come out of the room, the way you've been starting to, and there's real risk.

Abby: I don't like it in my room anymore. I don't like it that my best friend hasn't thought of me in five years.

Dr. Leibowitz: Abby, you looked me up in the phone book. You made that first call. That was an act of real courage and determination. That was the act of someone who needs more than her bedroom, more than her imagination.

Abby: What if they hate me?

Dr. Leibowitz: Obviously, I don't think they do. But if I'm wrong, and they do hate you, then it's probably best for you to find out now, when you're in therapy, when you'll be going to college in a year and a half, than some other time. Jess found out when she was very young, and we know what it did to her. Jocelyn is just finding out now, and she can't handle it.

Abby: And I can?

Dr. Leibowitz: Yes.

Abby: You sound so sure.

Dr. Leibowitz: I've been thinking about this a lot, you know—breakfast is the most important meal of the day. What you need to do, for everybody's sake, is minimize the risk.

Abby: You mean I don't just fling myself into their arms and tell them I love them.

Dr. Leibowitz: Good thinking. Now which one of your parents is most approachable?

Abby: Great. The python or the tiger.

Dr. Leibowitz: Abby, they are human beings.

Abby: My mother. Not by much, but at least she isn't always telling me how mediocre I am.

Dr. Leibowitz: Fine. Your mother. She would have been my choice too. I think you should start a conversation with your mother. A dialogue if you will. Talk to her.

Abby: About what?

147

Dr. Leibowitz: *You're the good listener. What do you think you should talk to her about?*

Abby: *You mean, I should talk to her about herself?*

Dr. Leibowitz: *If you talk to her about the rest of the family, you're taking much too much risk. It's too sensitive a topic for her. If you talk to her about the weather, you're not taking enough risk. You've had your share of please-pass-the-salt conversations. But have you ever given her the chance to tell you who she is, what she cares about?*

Abby: *You mean like, hi Mom, how's your life?*

Dr. Leibowitz: *Make up a list of questions. Ones whose answers would really interest you. Then tell her you want to interview her. She'll be flattered. People always are when someone shows interest in them.*

Abby: *Questions, not accusations.*

Dr. Leibowitz: *You got it.*

<u>Questions I'd Like Answers To</u>

1. Why do you like your job so much?
2. Why, if Dad's name is John and your name is Ginny and you named your other children Jocelyn, Jessica, and John Junior, am I named Abigail?
3. Were you close to your sister when you were growing up?
4. Why did you decide to become a lawyer?
5. Do you have affairs?

148

6. Do you still love Dad?

7. What's your favorite color, flower, food, season? What's your favorite any thing?

8. Did you love your parents?

9. If you were to die tomorrow, what would you most regret not having done?

10. Why, if you love me, don't you show it? And if you don't love me, why not?

Mar. 4
Dear Rachel,

Okay. They're loaded questions, a little more loaded than Dr. Leibowitz might like. But I don't have to ask all of them. I can pick and choose, seeing how the conversation goes.

Conversation. With my mother. What an idea!

Abby

Transcript: Conversation Between Abby Talbott and Her Mother

Abby: *Hi Mom, are you busy?*
Mom: *Well, actually . . .*
Abby: *The thing is I kind of have this assignment to interview you and I was wondering if we could do it now.*

149

Mom: *Is that what the tape recorder is for?*

Abby: *Yeah. It won't take too long, I promise.*

Mom: *All right. Let's get it over with.*

Abby: *Great. Now, for starters, your name is Ginny Leigh Talbott.*

Mom: *Virginia Leigh Talbott.*

Abby: *But everybody calls you Ginny.*

Mom: *The only people who call me Ginny are your father and our mutual friends. That's it. My family calls me Virginia, and so do my friends from school, and everybody at work. I'm surprised you thought people called me Ginny.*

Abby: *It's just you're Ginny and Dad's John and then there's Jocelyn and Jess and Johnny.*

Mom: *That wasn't my idea.*

Abby: *What do you mean?*

Mom: *When John and I met, he thought it would be cute if we were John and Ginny. Your father had a real fondness for cute in those days.*

Abby: *Dad?*

Mom: *I know. He lost a lot of that when Johnny died. He buried his heart that day. Anyway, he insisted on calling me Ginny, and to be honest, I thought it was cute too. Naturally, he was determined that his first son be named John. His grandfather was named John, and he worshiped him. But we had a girl, so we went with the other J name. Second time around, the same story. I started feeling overwhelmed with J-sounding names, but there was no going back. Finally Johnny was born and that was the end of that.*

Abby: *Did you think about giving me a J name when I was born?*

Mom: *No.*

Abby: *Why not?*

Mom: *For a couple of reasons. What kind of interview is this?*

150

Abby: *It's an assignment, Mom. What reasons?*

Mom: *I couldn't do it because of Johnny. And besides, I had a grandmother I wanted to name a daughter for. I'd wanted to name Jocelyn Abigail, but John said no, and he said no to naming Jess that as well, and you were my last chance.*

Abby: *I'm named for my grandmother?*

Mom: *Your great-grandmother. You didn't know that?*

Abby: *I don't think so.*

Mom: *I loved her. She was a wonderful woman, warm and affectionate. My own mother was nothing like that. She took after her father, a very strong person, but not the kind of person you go to for hugs. Don't tell me. I know I take after her. That's one reason why I loved my grandmother so deeply, because she was so much what I wanted to be and knew I never would be. My sister's much more like her. That's why I used to trust her with Jess. I felt maybe she could get through to Jess when I couldn't. It didn't work, but it was worth a try.*

Abby: *Were you and your sister close?*

Mom: *I idolized her. She was four years older than me, very warm, very popular. I was always Martha's kid sister, but it didn't bother me that much, maybe because of the age difference. You know, when I was little and my friends would come over, we'd make believe we were older girls, and I always pretended to be Martha. (laughs) I never told anybody that.*

Abby: *Did you have a lot of friends?*

Mom: *Up until high school. Then Martha went to college, and there were problems at home, and I withdrew, just pulled into my shell. I got great grades, all I ever did was study, and people thought of me as a grind, no fun, and never sought me out, which I took as rejection. I was class valedictorian, but I didn't have a date for the prom. So I decided if that was what my life was going to be like,*

151

then I'd make the most of it, just set aside my feelings and devote myself to my career. I'd be a lawyer, like my father. John and I met my second year of law school, and I refused to marry him until after I'd taken the bar exam, even though all I really wanted to do was get married and have children. At least that's what I kept telling myself at the time.

Abby: *You mean you were wrong?*

Mom: *Who's going to see this assignment of yours?*

Abby: *Don't worry. This is just raw data. I can censor it, if you want.*

Mom: *Off the record then?*

Abby: *Sure.*

Mom: *The minute I held Jocelyn in my arms, I realized it was a mistake, but there was no going back. And John was determined to have a son, so we tried again, and ended up with Jess. Jocelyn at least had been an easy baby. There was never a moment's peace with Jess, and Martha, who would have been the perfect mother, couldn't have children, and John was after me for another one, and all I wanted to do was find a nanny and start my career. Then I had Johnny, and God, it was like all my doubts just vanished. Part of it was John and the pleasure I took in his pleasure, but part of it was that baby. I . . . I'm sorry. I never talk about him. I can't.*

Abby: *Then you had me to replace him.*

Mom: *We thought . . . It was foolish of us. Every child is different. You'd think we would have learned that with Jocelyn and Jess.*

Abby: *Did you ever love me?*

Mom: *Of course I did. I do now. I'll always love you. You're my baby. God, Abby, am I that bad a mother?*

Abby: *No, of course not.*

Mom: *I know I'm not what . . . It's all style, you know. My style worked with Jocelyn, at least up until now, and noth-*

*ing would have worked with Jess, I really believe that, but
you, you were always so reserved, and I thought, well that's
good, she's self-sufficient, she can fend for herself, because
I had so little to give you, to give anybody, after Johnny,
and then Martha and Mike moved away, and Jess became
even harder, and . . . I'm sorry. I know this is an assignment, but I don't want to talk about it anymore.*

Abby: *Mom, I do love you.*

Mom: *Yes, thank you, please leave me alone now, all
right?*

Questions I'd Like Answers To - Dad

1. What does it feel like, saving lives?

2. How is it you could love Johnny so deeply and everybody else (except maybe Jocelyn) so little?

3. Are you like your father?

4. Do you have affairs?

5. Do you still love Mom?

6. When you saw I was a girl, did you decide that very moment that I could be nothing but mediocre, or did it take you a week, a month, a year before you came to that conclusion?

7. If you were to die tomorrow, what would you most regret not having done?

8. Was there ever a moment when you felt proud of me? Did you ever once love me?

Transcript: Conversation Between Abby Talbott and Her Father

Abby: Hi Dad, are you busy?

Dad: Abby, I've put in a very hard week, and all I want to do now is relax and watch this basketball game.

Abby: It's an assignment. I have some questions I need to ask you, that's all.

Dad: What kind of assignment?

Abby: I'm supposed to interview you.

Dad: Get the hell out of here. I don't need this crap.

Abby: Dad . . .

Dad: You heard me. I want you out of here right now, and I don't want to see you for the rest of the day.

Abby: Dad, I have these questions I have to ask you.

Dad: What is that? A tape recorder. Give that thing to me.

Abby: No.

Dad: I said hand it over.

Abby: I will not. Dad, it's mine. You can't just take it. Dad, stop it!

Mar. 4
Dear Rachel,

I hate him. I hate him. I hate him. I hate him. I hate him. I hate him. I hate him. I hate him. I hate him. I hate him. I hate him. I hate him. I hate him. I hate him. I hate

Transcript: Session with Abby Talbott

Abby: . . . *and he took the recorder from me, just grabbed it from my hand, and threw it across the room. It hit the wet bar and broke.*
Dr. Leibowitz: *How did you feel?*
Abby: *Terrified. Furious. I wanted to kill him. I wanted to die.*
Dr. Leibowitz: *What did you do?*
Abby: *I ran out of there. I couldn't go to Mom, I don't even think she was in, so I went to my bathroom and I locked the door.*
Dr. Leibowitz: *Did you think your father was going to harm you?*
Abby: *I didn't know what to think. I was too scared. If I'd been Jess, yeah, he would have gone after me.*
Dr. Leibowitz: *With Jess, it would have escalated into violence.*
Abby: *Yeah.*
Dr. Leibowitz: *But with you, it didn't.*
Abby: *After a while, I felt pretty stupid in the bathroom, so I got out, and I went back to the family room and peeked in. Dad was watching the basketball game, just like nothing had happened. I hated him more that moment than I ever have before.*
Dr. Leibowitz: *Why?*
Abby: *I was nothing to him. Absolutely nothing. Jocelyn he*

would have spoken to, and Jess he would have hurt, but me . . . (cries)

Dr. Leibowitz: *Would you have preferred it if he had hurt you? If instead of breaking the tape recorder, he'd hit you?*

Abby: *(cries) No. Why should I want that?*

Dr. Leibowitz: *It's a form of attention.*

Abby: *I hate him. (cries)*

Dr. Leibowitz: *After you looked in on him, what did you do?*

Abby: *I went back to my room, and I stayed there the rest of the day. I didn't even come out for supper.*

Dr. Leibowitz: *Why? Were you afraid to see him?*

Abby: *I don't know. I just wasn't hungry.*

Dr. Leibowitz: *If you'd been hungry, would you have gone out?*

Abby: *I don't know. Why? Did I do something wrong? Was it my fault? (cries)*

Dr. Leibowitz: *No, of course not. Your father is an angry, violent man, and at least for the time being, you're stuck with him. But I don't want to see you punishing yourself because of that.*

Abby: *(cries)*

Dr. Leibowitz: *That was Saturday. How were things on Sunday?*

Abby: *Saturday night there was a five-car pileup. He went back to the hospital around midnight, and I didn't see him again until Monday morning. How can he do that? How can he be so cruel, such a monster, and then work so hard to save people's lives?*

Dr. Leibowitz: *Maybe that's the only time he feels good about himself.*

Abby: *He'd be right too. (laughs and cries)*

Transcript: Session with Abby Talbott

Dr. Leibowitz: *Have you seen much of your father since last Saturday?*

Abby: *Not much. But I've been thinking about him a lot.*

Dr. Leibowitz: *What kind of thoughts?*

Abby: *Not homicidal, if that's what you're worrying about. (laughs) No, I remembered something Jess wrote me, about how she was sure Dad would die before he was sixty.*

Dr. Leibowitz: *How old is he now?*

Abby: *Fifty-two. So I guess I'm stuck with him for another eight years.*

Dr. Leibowitz: *Are you worried that he's going to die soon?*

Abby: *I don't know. Sometimes that's what I want, and sometimes I think about how I just can't picture him living like he does forever. He's all work and anger, that's his whole world, and it isn't like his work is easy.*

Dr. Leibowitz: *Do you feel sorry for him?*

Abby: *No. I don't. It's his choice.*

Dr. Leibowitz: *But it still bothers you.*

Abby: *He's my father. And it scares me. Don't girls marry men like their fathers?*

Dr. Leibowitz: *Not always. Your father is an abusive man. You know that, and you know how much that hurts. I think you'll be forewarned and choose not to marry a man like him.*

Abby: *Jocelyn didn't. Roger's a marshmallow.*

Dr. Leibowitz: *You can probably find someone in between if you're willing to do some looking.*

Abby: *What if he died tomorrow? What if he had a heart attack or a stroke or drove into a tree or . . . (cries)*

Dr. Leibowitz: *I have a friend who believes in resolutions. She thinks everything can be resolved, that there don't have to be any loose ends, that life's a book with chapters and The End printed neatly on the last page. I keep telling her*

157

she's wrong (not that she asks), that there isn't a neat resolution for everything, that some feelings always stay unresolved, that life is filled with murky waters.

Abby: (laughs) The two of you must have some great conversations.

Dr. Leibowitz: (laughs) My point is . . .

Abby: Your point is Dad could die tomorrow, he could die ten years from tomorrow, he could die when I'm ninety-two, and he'll always scare me and I'll always hate him.

Dr. Leibowitz: No, that isn't my point.

Abby: Sorry.

Dr. Leibowitz: My point is no matter when your father dies, you're going to have mixed feelings about him. You don't want him to die now. If you did, you wouldn't have cried at the thought. Jess doesn't want him to die now either. She wants to prove to him she can make something of her life in spite of him. Jocelyn doesn't want him to die now. She wants to show him his first grandchild. But all of you hate him and fear him, just as you love him, and long for his love.

Abby: If I could have chosen my parents, I would have picked such different ones.

Dr. Leibowitz: It doesn't work that way. You can have some control over friends and lovers and husbands, but almost none over parents and siblings and children.

Abby: So I have to learn to live with what I have.

Dr. Leibowitz: The key word there is live.

Transcript: Session with Abby Talbott

Abby: I thought about what you said about my father. On my own time.

Dr. Leibowitz: Did you come to any conclusions?

158

Abby: *I don't know if conclusions is the right word. I thought about how I'd feel if he did just die, no warning, right now.*

Dr. Leibowitz: *How did you feel about that?*

Abby: *You're asking prompting questions again. And I don't need them today.*

Dr. Leibowitz: *Sorry. Force of habit.*

Abby: *I thought about how I mostly hate him, because he mostly hates me, and he hates me because I wasn't a son, I wasn't a second Johnny, and I hate him because he's cruel and unloving and he'll never be the father I want and I hate him for that. And I thought well that's great, we're just going to hate each other forever because I guess I'll hate him even after he's dead. But there were times when I didn't hate him and there were even times when he didn't hate me, and that doesn't make things any easier, if you know what I mean.*

Dr. Leibowitz: *I think I do.*

Abby: *This morning I got up to make myself breakfast, and Dad was in the kitchen pouring himself some coffee, he lives on stimulants, and I don't know, something just came over me, maybe it was even pity, but I just looked at him and I said, you know Dad I loved that dollhouse you gave me. Just like that.*

Dr. Leibowitz: *You didn't plan on saying it.*

Abby: *I didn't plan on saying anything. I never talk to Dad in the morning, and that's when we mostly see each other. But this morning I said that about the dollhouse, and first Dad looked at me like I was crazy, what dollhouse, what the hell was I talking about, but then, I don't know, maybe the caffeine kicked in, but he said, I remember that, God I was up all night putting that damn thing together, and then you thought Santa brought it to you. And I said, yeah, but it took a surgeon's hands to assemble it, and he said, a surgeon's hands and the patience of a saint, and then*

159

he laughed. He actually laughed and I laughed too, and he said, glad you liked it, but don't expect me to make you another one.

Dr. Leibowitz: *Was he laughing then?*

Abby: *No.*

Dr. Leibowitz: *(laughs)*

Abby: *I know. But now I have that moment. I have that laugh. I'm never going to get much from my parents. Mom could teach me about fortress building, and Dad . . . But he laughed. You know. He laughed.*

March 25
Dear Rachel,

You probably don't remember me. We met several summers ago, when our families stayed at the same hotel. For a week, we were best friends, and then we all went home. I wrote to you a few times, and you wrote back once or twice, but we haven't seen each other since, and I doubt you've thought about me.

So you're probably wondering why I'm writing. In a way, I'm wondering too, but it's been on my mind to do it, and I decided today was as good a time as any.

I don't know if you could tell it then, but I was very unhappy and my family was too. In a lot of ways, we still are. One of the things I liked so much about you that week was your family was also having problems. It made me feel less alone.

When I wrote to you and you didn't write back, I kept on writing letters, addressing them to you but never mailing them. After a while, those letters evolved into my diary, and I wrote them several times a week, or whenever I needed to confide in someone. Instead of writing Dear Diary though, I kept on writing Dear Rachel. Naturally, after a while I didn't think of you as I wrote, but it was easier for me, felt more natural, to keep addressing the entries to you.

160

Right before Christmas this year, I tried to kill myself. I was found, and there wasn't any permanent damage, but I did succeed in scaring myself into therapy. I see a psychologist twice a week, and I feel better about myself than I ever have. I feel a lot less desperate than I was before. Sometimes I'm even hopeful about my future. I think, I don't have to keep myself locked in. I can reach out to people, real people. I have worth.

I've been writing in my journal less and less lately. I don't think I'll give it up, but I'm starting to think about talking to real people instead of imaginary ones. That's one reason why I'm writing, to write to the real Rachel, rather than the one I've been pouring out all my troubles to all these years.

The second reason is to thank you for the use of your name, but I think from now on, my journal's just going to be a journal—letters to myself and no one else. I don't think I need the Rachel that you never really were anymore.

And finally, I want to thank you for being the Rachel you really were back then when we met. There isn't much in my life I can look back on as simply being pleasant, and I can that week, and that's largely because of you.

I hope your life is going well. I really hope that for you, just as I'm starting to hope that for myself.

Sincerely,
Abby Talbott

April 2
Dear Johnny,

Well, it's been ten years since you dropped in last, and I thought I'd catch you up on what's been going on.

Jocelyn's pregnant. She called last week to tell us. Due date is November 1. Dad was furious at first, and Mom

161

was cool, but Jocelyn just plowed through, announcing that she and Roger and the baby would be here for Thanksgiving, so we should start making plans. She told Dad if it was a boy, they were definitely going to name him John, but they hadn't decided yet on a girl's name. Dad said he knew better than to expect a grandson. I'm not sure, but it's possible he meant that as a joke.

Jess is serving her prison sentence. The funny thing is, she might get paroled in time for Thanksgiving. What a scene that could be! She writes me occasionally, but she stays in closer touch with Jocelyn. She's been going to AA meetings and she says for the first time ever she's thinking about what a straight life might be like without it terrifying her. I still have trouble realizing how scared Jess is all the time, but she is, more even than me.

My life's been pretty shaky over the past ten years, but I'm starting to think it could have a happy ending. I tried to kill myself a few months ago, and when I thought I was dying, I reached out to you, but you weren't there. I like to think you didn't want me to die just yet, and that's why you didn't hold your hand out to mine.

I think about you a lot, Johnny, who you were, even who you would have been. I know I'm alive only because you died, and lately I've been thinking that means I owe you something. I owe you a valuable life. I used to think you would have had things so easy if you'd lived, Mom and Dad just adored you, but maybe I've overrated what their love could do, since I've had so little of it. Maybe it would have been as hard for you to live with their expectations as it has been for me to live without them. And maybe you weren't perfect after all, just a cute smart little boy who never had a chance to disappoint them.

I'm sorry I never knew you. I've always been glad you visited me that day. It made me feel special, and I'm grateful to you for that.

I've thought a lot about this letter, and what I was going to do with it. The way I see it, there's a double whammy against your actually reading it. First of all, you're dead, and second, you died before you ever learned to read (even in the family legend of Johnny, nobody's claimed you could read at age two).

So what I've decided to do is burn the letter, and then take the ashes and a rose (a red one—you must be bored with white ones by now) to your grave, and leave them there. I sense somehow that even if you can't read a letter, you can read the ashes of one.

Wish me well, Johnny. Say your prayers for me, as I say mine for you.

Love,
Your sister,
Abby

The Most Important Event in My Life
by Abigail Leigh Talbott

I used to think life was whole, a unit, perfectly formed and impenetrable, and that I stood outside life, and therefore must be dead.

But now I know that life is just fragments, a little piece of love, a sliver of anger, emotions, events, desires, and failures, cosmic dust in the ocean of the universe. There is a whole, but we are all part of it, and pain should not be mistaken for death.

Today in history class, Mr. Lopez assigned us group projects, six in all, and he said we should choose our own groups. I sat for a moment paralyzed as the other kids, all of whom seemed more confident, more

163

socialized than me, formed the groups that they wanted.

But then I turned to Tim, a boy who sits next to me, and I said, may I join your group? and he said great, I was hoping you would ask, and once again and for the first time, I realized I was inside that ocean universe, filled with love and fear, longing and satisfaction, and finally I knew how to float.

ABOUT THE AUTHOR

SUSAN BETH PFEFFER graduated from New York University with a degree in television, motion picture, and radio studies. She is the author of the highly praised *The Year Without Michael,* an ALA Best Book for Young Adults and a *Publishers Weekly* Best Book of the Year, and many other acclaimed young adult novels, including *About David, Fantasy Summer, Getting Even,* and *Most Precious Blood.*

Susan Beth Pfeffer is a native New Yorker who currently resides in Middletown, New York.